"ARE YOU A SPY?"

"I have no intention of sati Miss Traherne," he replied calm a panther's grace. "I believe you wished your gown undone?"

There was a gleam in those dark blue eyes, and Elizabeth began to back away hastily. She took no more than two steps, when he caught her, his cool, impersonal hands holding her prisoner and making her uncomfortably aware of just how helpless she was. The heavy curtain of hair was moved gently out of the way, and she felt his hands deftly undo the recalcitrant buttons. A moment later the dress was loose, the hands released her, and she jumped away as if burned.

Very dangerously attractive, she thought absently, staring up at that dark face for a long, breathless minute. "I . . . thank you," she stammered, and was surprised to see a small smile quirk his mouth.

"My pleasure, Miss Traherne." The low voice was curiously caressing. "Any time."

Other Anne Stuart Titles by Bell Bridge Books:

Historical Romance

Lady Fortune

Barrett's Hill

Prince of Magic

The Demon Count Novels

Romantic Suspense

Nightfall

Shadow Lover

Now You See Him

The Catspaw Collection

The Houseparty

by

Anne Stuart

Bell Bridge Books

This is a work of fiction. Names, characters, places and incidents are either the products of the author's imagination or are used fictitiously. Any resemblance to actual persons (living or dead), events or locations is entirely coincidental.

B

Bell Bridge Books
PO BOX 300921
Memphis, TN 38130
Print ISBN: 978-1-61194-668-0

Bell Bridge Books is an Imprint of BelleBooks, Inc.

Copyright © 1985 by Anne Kristine Stuart Ohlrogge writing as Anne Stuart

Published in the United States of America.

All rights reserved. No part of this book may be reproduced in any form or by any electronic or mechanical means, including information storage and retrieval systems, without permission in writing from the publisher, except by a reviewer, who may quote brief passages in a review.

A mass market edition of this book was published as a Fawcett Crest Book, published by Ballantine Books in 1985

We at BelleBooks enjoy hearing from readers.
Visit our websites
BelleBooks.com
BellBridgeBooks.com
ImaJinnBooks.com

10 9 8 7 6 5 4 3 2 1

Cover design: Debra Dixon
Interior design: Hank Smith
Photo/Art credits:
Garden © Mark Smith | Dreamstime.com
Woman (manipulated) © Arturkurjan | Dreamstime.com

:Lhpo:01:

Chapter 1

IT WAS A COOL, sunny afternoon in late winter, and somewhere in London two gentlemen met in an unprepossessing little room that may or may not have been part of the offices necessary to the running of a large and disorderly regency. There were no paintings on the walls, but the desk between the two men was a massive piece of furniture reserved for those in power, and the elderly gentleman who sat at it stared with unseeing eyes at the cool, handsome face of the young man.

"I cannot like this situation, my boy," Sir Henry Hatchett was saying gruffly. "It ain't right to involve civilians in this sort of affair. No matter how careful we are, we can't control everything all the time. I gather Jeremy Traherne's brother and sister will be at Winfields for this houseparty."

"Surely we can count on them for assistance?" the younger man questioned swiftly.

"If we had to. But you know Traherne would never forgive us if anything happened to his family. He's making sacrifices enough for the cause. As you are, dear boy. There's a limit to how much martyrdom the Crown has a right to demand."

The word the younger man used was short and satisfyingly blasphemous. "If you were to ask Jeremy, he would tell you, as I do, that it's hardly a case of martyrdom; it's more in the nature of a challenge. You haven't heard me complain, and you're not about to. I understand your reservations about this houseparty, but tell me, sir, do we really have any other choice?"

Sir Henry sighed. "I'm afraid not. We'll simply have to be very careful, very careful indeed. A great deal is riding on this. The work of a year, at the very least. We simply cannot have it all go for naught."

"We shan't fail, sir."

Sir Henry eyed the coolly determined young soldier opposite him. "I would guess that you won't object too strenuously to having this over and done with, would you, lad?"

"I won't deny it's been damnably uncomfortable on occasion," he agreed with an unexpected flash of humor. "Though I'd do it again if the situation warranted it."

"Aye, I'm sure you would. If it weren't for men like you and Jeremy Traherne, we'd have lost out to Bonaparte years ago."

The younger man dismissed the praise with a shrug. "Tell me, sir, do you have any reason to fear we might not succeed this time?"

"None at all," Sir Henry replied. "But I wish to hell it were over with. I won't rest easy until we have that scheming traitor brought to justice. When I think of the number of our lads who've lost their lives because of his vanity and greed, I feel frankly murderous."

"I don't blame you. But it shan't happen again. By this time on Monday our traitorous friend will be as harmless as . . . as Jeremy Traherne's sister."

Sir Henry allowed himself a small smile. "Obviously you haven't met the girl yet. According to Traherne, she's a real corker. I only hope she won't make matters more difficult. We can't afford to take her into our confidence, and I couldn't be responsible for her life if she were to find out what's going on at Winfields."

"Is there any reason she should?"

"Traherne says she's the very devil. Bright, inquisitive, and far too pretty. She was the one who found LeBoeuf, you know. Damnable luck!"

"I gather Jeremy knows she and his brother will be involved, then."

"He knows. And he doesn't like it," Sir Henry said in his gloomiest tone of voice. "But he agrees with us; there's no way to avoid it. I only hope things work out as we've planned."

The younger man's expression was grim, and Sir Henry, watching it in the fading afternoon light, felt vaguely nervous. And profoundly grateful that he was on their side and not that of the Corsican monster.

"They will," the young man said in a steely voice.

And Sir Henry had little doubt that they would.

"MY DEAR SUMNER," Elizabeth Traherne began in her well-modulated voice, "I still fail to see why we must spend the entire time with the squire. You know that his mother doesn't really care for us, and as for Cousin Adolphus himself, why, I am certain he invites us under duress and not for any desire for our lively company. Couldn't we possibly cry off this time?"

It was later that same afternoon on a winter's day, and Elizabeth had been so bold as to accost her brother in his study at the drafty old parsonage. Of all the pleasant, well-lit rooms this was the most pleasant, and Elizabeth's brother had unhesitatingly chosen it for his own. The roaring fire filled the farthest corners with heat, the winter sunlight poured in the windows, and the book-lined walls provided a perfect background to her brother's elegant figure—a background he had cultivated deliberately.

The Very Reverend Sumner Traherne cast a disapproving look out of his large, melting blue eyes, craned his neck in an effort to appear magisterial, and made a reproving sound in his throat, which, though undeniably mellifluous, was somewhat reminiscent of a boar in rut.

"You are frivolous and ungrateful, Elizabeth," he said sternly, folding his well-shaped hands across his knee. "Cousin Adolphus invites us only for our pleasure and to show me some distinguishing attention. He was so condescending as to confide his wish that you, my girl, would receive some much needed brightening of your downcast spirits. He's fully aware of the strain of the last few months, without a word from Jeremy. And your finding that drowned French sailor down at Starfield Cove scarcely helped the tone of your spirits."

Elizabeth allowed herself a momentary shudder as the memory of those blank, unseeing eyes intruded. "That unpleasant experience was hardly my fault, Sumner."

"I am not suggesting that it was. Though why you have to ride such great distances is beyond my comprehension. Still, you never were a biddable female. And little does Adolphus realize that your supposed meekness is merely the mask for the most unseeming levity, usually at his expense. May I remind you—"

"Whether you may or not is beside the point," she interrupted with a sigh. "I wish you wouldn't prose on so."

Again that snort issued forth from Sumner's broad chest. "Adolphus Wingert, besides being a cousin of ours, is the squire of this area, the justice of the peace, and our most generous patron. It would behoove you to show more gratitude and respect."

"I'm certain his mother would prefer that I show my respect from a distance," she murmured, unrepentant.

"And I cannot imagine what you have against Lady Elfreda. She has been all that is kind."

"She is afraid, my sweet brother, that I mean to run off with her overfed, overbearing son. It is incomprehensible to her that any female could find Adolphus something less than the embodiment of girlish dreams." She allowed herself a faint shudder.

"I would have thought you'd be a bit past girlish dreams," he stated with a brotherly lack of tact. "As a matter of fact, Adolphus called you a very fetching young lady. You could go a lot farther and do a lot worse than marry someone like Adolphus Wingert."

"Why, Sumner." Elizabeth's eyes opened wide with surprise tinged with amusement. "I wonder that you would countenance the thought of my marrying with such equanimity. I had presumed you were expecting me to devote my life to you."

"Naturally," Sumner responded with his usual gravity. "However, an alliance with the Wingert family could only benefit my career in the long run and would do Jeremy no harm, either. And I have little doubt Adolphus would be generous enough to see to a housekeeper for me, should he decide that you might suit."

Elizabeth bit back the retort that threatened to bubble over. She tried to allow herself only one biting remark an hour, and she already had overstepped her allowance. She sighed and tried again. "I am very sensible of the honor Adolphus does me," she said meekly enough, "though I doubt there is anything serious in his attentions. And I wonder whether it is truly Christian of us, Sumner, to burden poor Lady Elfreda with worry for naught," she added. "You cannot argue that she wouldn't rather see Adolphus married to a lady of title or at least someone a bit more biddable. And a slightly more noble lineage wouldn't .hurt matters, either."

"There's nothing wrong with our lineage," her brother said abruptly, his handsome face set in an intimidating frown that left Elizabeth unmoved. "The Trahernes are one of the oldest families in all Britain."

"Yes, but our ancestors were Welsh."

Sumner did not care to have disagreeable facts clouding his pontifications. "One of the oldest families in Britain," he repeated firmly. "And your portion is very nice indeed. Not that the Wingerts would have any need of your dowry, and I wouldn't doubt that Adolphus might be generous enough to turn it over to the church."

And its current incumbent, Elizabeth added silently, accustomed to her brother's itchy palms. "I wouldn't rely on any future match, Sumner. I am hardly the type to suit Adolphus Wingert, you must admit."

For once her brother was tactful. Elizabeth could well imagine what he was thinking. Not that she was a bad-looking female, of course. How could she be, when she and her two brothers were known as the dashing Trahernes among their set? If nature had unfairly given her brothers the more spectacular good looks, she hadn't come out badly in the end, either. Without a doubt she was what might be termed a handsome young woman. Although a bit above average height, she still had the innate good sense not to tower over the majority of the gentlemen she met. Her rich chestnut hair was streaked from the sun, for she would go out hatless in their back garden despite Sumner's remonstrations. That same reckless disregard for the sun accounted for the faint spattering of freckles across her delicate nose that were still in evidence in late March. Her eyes were a warm, laughing brown, although that laughter could have an uncomfortable edge to it. Her chin and her nature were too willful, and of course she was far too opinionated and intelligent for a woman.

But then, she took very good care of Sumner, and he wasn't one to be ungrateful. He knew that he was a lucky man to have his only sister devote her life to his wellbeing, and it was a fortunate thing that she'd never evinced any interest in the admittedly small number of suitable gentlemen who had come her way. If truth be told, Sumner had done his share to discourage them once Jeremy had left for the war. Elizabeth had allowed him to do so, leaving him secure in the belief that she would be far more content managing a parsonage than she would be gallivanting in the dissipated pleasures of London with some rackety gentleman.

But it appeared that Sumner's forbearance was coming to an end. In the case of Adolphus Wingert, he'd clearly decided to nobly put someone else's comfort above his own. Balanced against the good it would do his career, it wasn't wise to be too selfish. Therefore, he eyed his sister and granted her his most encouraging smile, one she distrusted above all things.

"I am certain that Adolphus could not help but appreciate a treasure such as you, my dear," he said smoothly.

"And I am sure you must have windmills in your head, Sumner," she replied frankly. "And I shan't have you encouraging that great lummox. For the time being I am quite content taking care of my dear brother."

"For the time being?" he echoed in a hollow voice. "But what else could you possibly want to do?"

"Well, I don't expect you to end your days a bachelor, dear heart. Already you have half the ladies in the congregation swooning. Sooner or later some enterprising damsel will catch sight of that golden head of curls and that handsome face, and you'll find yourself leg shackled before you know it."

"I have no immediate plans," said Sumner, not at all displeased with this summing up of his not inconsiderable physical attractions.

"But you never know what might happen. And I doubt that your bride would care to have a managing sister-in-law about the place. So I thought I might keep house for Jeremy when he returns." A troubled look clouded her expressive face. "I suppose I should say if he returns."

"Don't be absurd, of course the boy will return," Sumner said gruffly. "Our brother leads a charmed life. Three years fighting Napoleon and not even a scratch on him."

"I trust you are right," Elizabeth said with a sigh.

"And I would think he'd be just as likely to marry as I am. He always had an eye for a pretty girl."

"If and when he does, I have other options. It is entirely possible I might still get married. I am only twenty-three. Rather ancient by some standards, but I might still be able to attract an eligible party, someone a bit more appealing than Cousin Adolphus. A widower, perhaps, or an aging cleric. I've certainly had a great deal of experience managing a vicar's household. Or I might set up house on my own. There is more than enough money for it, and I might even have Miss Biddleford to keep me company."

"Miss Biddleford is a shameless bluestocking with the most dangerous ideas. I blame having her as your governess for all the flighty and, yes, seditious ideas that racket around in your brain."

"Sumner, you're a shocking prig," Elizabeth shot back cheerfully. "How could I have such a conservative brother? Of course, Biddy's to blame for my outrageous opinions."

"Well, I shan't allow you to set up house with her. I've never heard of anything so ridiculous in my entire life," Sumner announced, leaning back in his chair with a decisive air.

Elizabeth smiled sweetly. "My dear Sumner, you won't have any say in the matter. If you remember, my money was left entirely in my hands, not in yours or Jeremy's. You have no say over it or me."

"Father must have been demented when he wrote that will," he said, fretting. "Imagine stating that you were better equipped to handle finances than your brothers."

"But you must admit I immediately gave you control of

your portion," she said demurely.

He eyed her with his usual misgivings. "I am not happy with you, Elizabeth. Your uncharitable attitude toward the Wingerts, your threats of disgracing yourself by running off on your own . . . I am deeply troubled."

For all Elizabeth's mischief making, she had a kind heart, and she reached out and touched one of Sumner's strong, elegantly shaped hands that had never known a day's hard work. "Don't fret yourself, Sumner. As long as you keep from meddling with Adolphus Wingert, I will restrain my wanderlust until Jeremy comes back. We've rubbed along very well together the past three years, and I am perfectly content. But I will tell you one last time: I have no wish to marry our portly cousin." This was said with a great deal of kindness accompanied by a sternness that brooked no argument, and as usual Sumner capitulated in the face of a stronger will than his own.

"Very well," he said somewhat sulkily. "It is your life, I suppose. Though how you can whistle such an advantageous match down the wind is more than I can understand. Haven't you any loyalty? Think what it could mean to my career."

"My dear, I would immolate myself for you, slave for you, manage your household and your accounts, counsel your parishioners, lead your choir, and write your sermons, but I will not marry Adolphus Wingert."

"You don't write my sermons," he said, hotly. "You may make a few suggestions and help with the phrasing and such, but the main kernel of thought is my own, and it is up to me which of your flighty suggestions I might possibly heed." Sumner's angelically beautiful face was red with annoyance, and his blue eyes with their absurdly long lashes were narrowed in fury.

"Of course, Sumner," Elizabeth said meekly, cursing once more her unruly tongue for speaking the unpalatable truth. "I didn't mean to suggest otherwise."

She could tell by his sly expression that her brother had recognized her contrition and intended to make full use of it. "Then you will agree to accompany me to Winfields? It should be charming—only family, Lady Elfreda tells me. Her brother-in-law, the general, might be there, with a few close friends. It should be a delightful time."

"Delightful," Elizabeth echoed gloomily. "I presume you mean Sir Maurice Wingert? The only thing more tedious than aging politicians is aging soldiers."

"Sir Maurice is one of our great heroes," Sumner said repressively. "You are totally lacking in respect, Elizabeth."

"I know." She sighed. "And I presume he'll have the usual complement of stiff young men to cater to his every whim."

"Oh, doubtless. He's got a new one, not that wispy fellow who couldn't even ride properly." Sumner snorted, his one real talent being horsemanship. "Come on, old girl, it'll do us some good. Keep us from worrying about Jeremy."

A shadow crossed Elizabeth's face. "Why haven't we heard from him, Sumner?"

"You know as well as I that he quite often doesn't get the chance to write nowadays. This wretched undercover work requires that we be kept completely in the dark. I don't like it, but what can we do?"

"Nothing, I suppose." She rose from her cramped, uncomfortable chair. There was only one decent seat in the room, and Sumner, of course, had claimed that as his own. "Shall I see to tea?" she inquired, suddenly ravenous. Sumner, like herself, was fond of food, although he never seemed to add an ounce to his trim frame, whereas her robust health had an unfortunate tendency to become a mite too robust on occasion.

"I trust we'll have more than dried-out salt biscuits," he remarked somewhat pettishly. "If you need to slim down, I fail to see why I too must suffer."

"There's a great deal to be said for mortifying the flesh," she replied limpidly. "I've had Mrs. Gibson make up a fresh batch of ginger biscuits. Six for you, six for me."

"Unfair!"

"It is perfectly fair," she said cheerfully. "I cannot resist temptation; therefore, temptation must be removed from my path and perforce from yours too. You wouldn't wish me to arrive at Winfields rivaling poor Adolphus in my girth, would you?"

"Two days will hardly give you enough time to put on that much," he muttered, scattering papers with a petulant shove. He was a man who liked his creature comforts.

"Well, then, why don't you speak to Mrs. Gibson and have her bring you some nice warm scones in your study later on? As long as I am unaware of their existence, I shan't mind," she allowed graciously.

"I fail to see why I must hide away in my study to eat," he cried. "Who runs this house, anyway?"

"I do."

He paused, nonplussed. "Well, who is the master of it, then?"

She dropped a kiss on the noble brow that had caused more than one susceptible parishioner to entertain lustful thoughts. "I am," she said, and whisked herself out the door, leaving her brother fuming, determined to sulk in his study until she returned to beg his pardon. But five minutes later, with visions of hot buttered scones and fresh ginger biscuits dancing in his head, he strode into the warm and cozy little drawing room that was Elizabeth's particular retreat. He found his sister curled up on the love seat by the fire, her feet tucked under her, a French novel of dubious social merit in one hand and a cup of tea nearly finished by her side. On the plate in front of her were two solitary-looking ginger biscuits.

Sumner eyed her with great sadness. "You promised me six," he said incomprehensibly, and then she realized that he meant the biscuits. She smiled up at him with that lightning change of expression that turned her face from passably pretty to almost beautiful.

"Not to worry, Sumner. I had Mrs. Gibson hide them from me. I'm sorry I teased you, dearest. I will go to Winfields. I will be on my best behavior, and you'll have no cause to blush for me."

Settling down opposite her, he eyed her warily. "And you won't set Adolphus's back up?" he questioned warily.

She handed him his tea. "I will flirt just the proper amount with Adolphus. I will convince Lady Elfreda of my disinterest. I will be respectful to Sir Maurice, polite to the boring young adjutant. Was there anyone else?"

"Miss O'Shea," he said, and his sister didn't miss the slight change in his mellifluous voice.

"I will be charming and friendly to Brenna O'Shea, with just the proper hint of condescension since she is a poor relation. That's what you wish, isn't it?" she inquired impishly.

"It is not! Miss O'Shea is a very nice young lady who thinks just as she ought about all things. You could take a lesson or two in deportment from her," he replied defensively.

The smile lit Elizabeth's golden-brown eyes once more. "I will study Miss O'Shea's behavior that I might learn proper deportment, and I will keep my tongue in my head at all times. What more could you ask, Sumner dear?"

He eyed her warily. "I could ask that there was even the slightest chance such a thing could happen. But the age of miracles has passed."

Elizabeth smiled. "Cheer up, Sumner. At the very worst, we are in for an extremely boring weekend. Nothing ever happens at Cousin Adolphus's houseparties. Nothing at all."

Chapter 2

Friday

WINFIELDS WAS A very ancient, very grand estate. The first Wingert had come over from France with William the Conqueror and had haughtily accepted as his due some fifty thousand of the ripest acres in Dorset. During the long centuries that followed, the Wingerts had erected Winfields, with each generation adding something to its overwhelming consequence and lack of beauty, till now it rambled and towered and loomed over the remaining five thousand acres (some of the Wingerts having been fatally addicted to gaming) with a ramshackle air that would have been comical had it not been for the sheer force of the Wingert family pride. The current incumbent, Baron Adolphus Wingert, squire of the village, justice of the peace, eligible bachelor and devoted son, spent as little time there as his duties would allow. But Adolphus was ever zealous in performing his duties, one of which was to entertain his distant cousin Sumner Traherne and that toothsome sister of his for a weekend just before the season started in London.

Another of his duties was to wed and beget an heir. His mother, the formidable Lady Elfreda Wingert, never failed to bring this up, and so at age forty Adolphus had finally decided to capitulate. With the right sort of female who knew better than to interfere in his life, he could continue on with his comfortable existence. The only question left was who the lucky girl would be.

There was Brenna, of course. When she had first arrived from Ireland to serve as his mother's companion, Adolphus had had little doubt she was one of his mother's selected brides. And indeed, she was a nice enough girl, biddable and sweet-tempered, but a bit on the bony side. Adolphus liked his females well rounded. His mind slipped back to Elizabeth Traherne, and he licked his thick, pink lips.

"Adolphus! His mother's piercing tones startled him out of a pleasant if somewhat lascivious reverie. With a great sigh and creaking of stays he rose from his comfortable chair and ambled off in the direction of that demanding voice.

It was a laborious process. Adolphus Wingert prided himself on his resemblance to his idol, the Prince Regent. Indeed, their girths were similar, with Adolphus having a slight edge. They had the same milky blue eyes, with golden waves trimmed and arranged a la Brutus. If Adolphus didn't affect quite the extremes of fashion Prinny was wont to, at least he was both colorful and elegant, and his stays were far tighter. Not only did the whalebone corseting hold his somewhat excessive stomach in check, it forced him to walk bolt upright, adding to the air of consequence he liked to affect. That it also interfered with his breathing, particularly after a heavy meal (and he ate no light ones), was merely one of the little annoyances one had to cope with in a less than perfect life.

By the time he traversed the hallway, descended three short steps, turned two sharp corners, and went up another four steps to his mother's salmon and apple-green sitting room, he was quite winded and had to content himself with staring, glassy-eyed, at his mother's indomitable figure.

Lady Elfreda Wingert was as spare as her only child was corpulent. She was fully six feet tall, with long, thin arms and strong hands that enjoyed pinching and slapping at the servants and her overgrown son, a narrow face adorned with a long, thin nose, two small, hard blue eyes, a thin-lipped mouth, and an expression of perpetual disapproval. Added to this unpleasant expression was an air of hauteur that was outdone only by her son. It was no wonder that the pretty young girl at her side had an unhappy expression lingering in eyes so green they could only be Irish.

"The Trahernes have arrived," she said in her cold, carrying tones. "I wonder if you know what absurd hopes you are encouraging in that young woman's breast by inviting them here every year. Soon she will be having airs above her station, fancying herself the future Lady Wingert, and I shall be forced to give her a sharp set down, making it impossible for me to attend my own church. Why you constantly refuse to listen to me is a wonder, when I have only your own best interests at heart."

"Now, now, Mama," he said soothingly between gasps for air. "Elizabeth is a very nice young lady. A less encroaching lady I have yet to find. Why, she even pretends that she has no interest in my attentions at all. How could one ask for more maidenly modesty?"

"Attentions?" Lady Elfreda had picked up the key word, and her voice rose sharply. "You haven't been paying her any marked attention, have you, Dolph?"

"Not yet," he admitted.

"Well, thank heavens for that. A more managing female I have yet to meet. If you wish to leg shackle yourself to an underbred, sharp-tongued hoyden who'd have you living under the cat's paw for the rest of your days, then I wash my hands of you. At age forty you should be old enough to know better."

"Now, Mama, you know I will be guided by your wise judgment in such matters," he said soothingly. "I would never willfully cause you any discomfort. But you wouldn't wish me to shirk my duty. The Trahernes are distant cousins, and I am Sumner's patron. It is necessary to entertain them occasionally, and what with Uncle Maurice arriving with his retinue, I couldn't think of a better time. Dispense with two duties at once, eh?"

"And that is another matter, Dolph. Out of the blue your uncle announces he is coming down to Winfields, without even asking whether or not it is convenient for us. And he's bringing not only that wretched young man I've heard so much about but a female besides! Some foreign woman. I told him he absolutely could not, but he ignored me. So like your dear father. I don't know what this world is coming to that I should have to entertain foreigners and poor relations at table, not to mention out-and-out traitors such as young Fraser. I can only thank heaven Sir Henry Hatchett and dear Beatrice chose this weekend to come also, or I might fear I'd be murdered in my bed. The next thing you know I'll be having the tenant farmers in for tea."

"Mama, I think you'd best watch your step about young Fraser. Nothing has been proved, you know. They would hardly have made him Uncle's adjutant if there was any blot on his record."

"They would hardly have made him your uncle's adjutant if there *weren't* a blot on his record. After his service in the Peninsula and the remarkable job he did in Vienna, there must be something terribly wrong for him to have been relegated to the position of high-class servant to an aging general. And I have little doubt you know exactly what it is," she added shrewdly.

"If I did, I would hardly be likely to spread such slander," said Adolphus loftily.

Lady Elfreda sighed, absently reaching out and giving her silent young companion a sharp pinch on the knee. "Help me to the front hall, Brenna," she ordered crisply. "Much as I dislike Miss Traherne, I suppose it would only lower myself to be petty and not welcome her."

"That's my dear mother," Adolphus said approvingly, nearly earning a pinch for himself. "And I'm certain you've judged Miss Traherne too harshly. She's a very charming young lady with just a trace too much liveliness of tongue."

THE LADY WITH the lively tongue was standing in the large, drafty front hall of Winfields, staring about her with undisguised amusement. "How anyone could want to live in such a place is beyond me," she whispered loudly to her brother as she grimaced at the lofty caverns above her. "I wouldn't be at all surprised if they have bats."

"Hush, Elizabeth!" Sumner hissed, holding his well-proportioned frame upright as his hosts approached with regal ceremony. "For once, try to make a good impression," he pleaded.

"Why?" she questioned in an undertone as the Wingert family reached them.

"Well, well, little Elizabeth," Adolphus said jovially. "You must allow me a cousin's prerogative." Before she could divine his intention, she found herself firmly seized and a great wet kiss planted just beneath her left eye. At the same time a pudgy hand happened to squeeze her breast. Before she could slap him, he moved nimbly out of reach, greeting her brother with a comradely condescension that never failed to grate on her nerves. Before she could regain her composure, a thin bejeweled hand was held out to her. She looked up into Lady Elfreda's lizard-like eyes with a small shudder of dismay. Belatedly she reached out to take the hand, and Lady Elfreda dropped it, leaving Elizabeth standing awkwardly with her hand outstretched, feeling, as always with that woman, clumsy and ill-bred.

"You haven't changed, dear Elizabeth," Lady Elfreda slid with a malicious smile. "How delightful that you could come to us for the weekend. Things get so tiresome this time of year, waiting for the season to begin." Before Elizabeth could reply, she sailed onward, greeting Sumner with the smile she reserved for handsome young men who treated her with the proper deference. Sumner knew the proper amount of flattery and shy respect to a nicety.

"Hallo, Elizabeth." Brenna's cool Irish voice broke through Elizabeth's irritation. "It's nice to see you again."

No warmth from this quarter, either, thought Elizabeth dolefully, eyeing the dark-haired, green-eyed little beauty in front of her with a hopeful smile. Brenna O'Shea had never shown any interest in Elizabeth's overtures of friendship during the six months she'd been in residence at Winfields, and by now Elizabeth had given up on her. Those green eyes only warmed, inexplicably, when they rested on her brother's admirable form.

The small, stilted group was moving into one of the more formal drawing rooms that were scattered around Winfields like a rabbit's warren, and there was nothing for Elizabeth to do but take up the rear, watching Brenna's slender little back with a twinge of jealousy. It must be nice to have a waist that was barely a man's hand span, she thought mournfully, fully aware that her own ripe curves constituted a more generous handful. Elizabeth sighed, seated herself as far from Lady Elfreda's disapproving attention but as near the tray of delicious cakes as possible, and accepted her fate.

Unfortunately, Adolphus had been watching both the cakes and Elizabeth closely. While his mother was distracted with serving the tea and evincing a proper interest in Sumner's charming anecdotes, the portly baron slipped to Elizabeth's side, a faint spattering of crumbs trailing across a baby-blue superfine jacket that had taken five ells to make up.

"What a treat to see you again, Cousin Elizabeth," he breathed. "And you're looking more stunning than ever. A fine, strapping figure of a girl," he said, licking his lips as if in anticipation of a tasty morsel.

Not this tasty morsel, thought Elizabeth firmly, giving him an unencouraging smile and edging as far away as the narrow chair would allow. "It's nice to see you again, Sir Adolphus," she replied distantly.

"Heavens, how formal we're being! You must call me Dolph, Cousin. After all, we're related."

"You are too kind, to call a mere connection a relationship," she said vaguely. "Your mother is looking well. You must be very fond of her." She could think of no reason for him to be, but Adolphus nodded sagely.

"A wonderful woman, my mother," he said. "But tell me about yourself, young lady. Any importunate young gentlemen hanging around, wishing to slip a ring on that pretty little hand?"

Elizabeth shuddered inwardly at the coy tone of voice as she glanced down at her strong, capable hands that were itching to box Adolphus's ears. "I am devoted to my brothers, as you know, Cousin," she said demurely. "Miss O'Shea is looking lovelier than ever," she added somewhat desperately.

His bulbous blue eyes never left her. "She's well enough," he replied, dismissing Brenna with one wave of a pudgy hand. "She hasn't your fire, my girl. And what's the news from that scamp Jeremy? Can we hope to see him soon?"

"Oh, I do hope so." Elizabeth sighed. "But we've had no definite word. I suppose that's just as well. We'd know soon enough if anything was wrong."

"Of course you would," he said soothingly, reaching out and patting her knee. He allowed his hand to rest there, and Elizabeth quickly shifted position, giving him an ingenuous smile as he was forced to move back. "Tell me, does that brother of yours allow you any freedom?"

"None at all," she replied quickly. "Sumner's a very high stickler. When is your uncle due?"

A shadow crossed his ruddy face. "Sometime this evening. I trust your brother has warned you about Michael Fraser?"

The name had a distant ring to it, but for the life of her Elizabeth couldn't remember the connection. "He may have done," she replied cautiously. "I'm afraid I don't remember. Who is Michael Fraser?"

"My uncle's current adjutant. He's from an old and proud Scottish family, younger son, I believe. A career man in the army and done well for himself and his country over the last years. Distinguished himself in the peninsular action and was considered quite promising in Vienna last year."

"Sounds estimable," Elizabeth said, stifling her yawn. "Just what a general's secretary should be."

"Not at all. Fraser was destined for much more important things than fetching and carrying for someone like Uncle Maurice, who's on the very edge of retiring. I don't know the details of it, but something very unpleasant happened after Vienna." Adolphus leaned closer, his breath hot on Elizabeth's averted cheek. "Nothing anyone could prove, I gather, because he wasn't clapped in irons. But it was a near thing."

Elizabeth's curiosity was piqued. "What sort of thing? Did he run off with his commander's wife, sell secrets to the French, seduce a duchess?" she questioned flippantly.

"I believe he was suspected of being a traitor," Adolphus whispered importantly. "But they couldn't prove a thing, so they had to settle for putting him in a post where he couldn't do any harm. Uncle Maurice hasn't many duties left to him in these last few months before he retires, and I doubt he'd have anything to do with military secrets of great importance. By the time he retires and Fraser gets reassigned, they should be able to get any proof they might need."

"Proof of what?" she inquired in a suitably hushed tone.

"I don't precisely know," Adolphus admitted fretfully, not liking to be in the dark any better than the inquisitive Elizabeth did. "Whether or not he's to be trusted, I suppose. More than one brave agent of our country has met his end by the traitor's hand. If there's any truth to the rumors surrounding Fraser, then he's a direct threat to people like your brother Jeremy. I would suggest you avoid him at all costs. There was no way I could keep him from coming, and of course it may all be a tempest in a teapot. He's a handsome enough devil," he added with a trace of envy in his voice. "You'd better keep an eye out for any blandishments, Cousin. Uncle Maurice should be able to keep things under control, and a friend of his from the Foreign Office is expected. We should be safe enough." He cast a nervous glance over his shoulder, as if he expected the villainous Fraser to appear with knife in hand.

Elizabeth's interest was well and truly caught by this time. "But why would he change sides? After having served king and country so well and truly for so long?"

Adolphus shrugged his thick shoulders, sending his highly starched shirt points into his ears with a sharp jab that caused tears of pain to start in those pale blue eyes. "Who can say what dark forces drive such men to desperate measures?" he intoned. "We can only guess at the tragic circumstances that affected him so—"

A small spurt of laughter from Elizabeth's tightly compressed lips drew his ruminations to an abrupt halt, and the expression in her golden-brown eyes was merry. "I never knew you were such a romantic, Adolphus! Michael Fraser sounds positively Byronic. I am quite looking forward to meeting this desperate traitor, tormented as he is by unspeakable horrors. Particularly if he's as devilishly handsome as you say he is."

Adolphus drew himself up, affronted. "You may very well laugh, Elizabeth, but I advise you to be careful. One man is dead already, do not forget, and I gather from friends of mine that the situation could still be dangerous."

Elizabeth's levity vanished abruptly. "A man dead?" she echoed. "You don't mean that French sailor?"

"Certain people think he was more than a mere sailor intent on smuggling laces and brandy," Adolphus announced. "The more I think about it, the more I am afraid that I may have been a bit hasty in ruling it death by misadventure. But then, as justice of the peace I have a great deal on my mind and can't be expected to be overly suspicious.

Chapter 3

AS ELIZABETH DRESSED for dinner that evening, she couldn't help but wonder why she was lavishing such special care on her toilette. She had been agreeably surprised by her choice of rooms this visit. Instead of the cramped little cubbyhole she'd endured on previous occasions, this time some kind hand (certainly not Lady Elfreda's or Brenna's) had given her a bright, airy room at the front of the house, complete with warm fire and a steaming hip bath awaiting her. On second thought, it might have been Lady Elfreda's poisonous touch. The room was as far away from Adolphus's master suite as could be managed, probably close to half a mile in this rambling place, Elizabeth thought gratefully. The baron's bulging blue eyes had a decidedly ravening look to them this time, a look Elizabeth couldn't fail to interpret; the farther away she was from his pudgy, grasping fingers, the better.

Surveying herself in the mirror, she could find no grievous fault, though perhaps she would have been wiser to have chosen something a bit less flattering. The high-waisted dress made the most of her elegant figure, and if it was a warm rose instead of her favorite green, well, she had enough sense to know that Brenna O'Shea had always chosen green for herself, and Elizabeth couldn't hope to outshine her diminutive beauty. At least the gown was silk, not the insipid muslins she'd been doomed to wear for the last five years, muslins that did absolutely nothing for her somewhat opulent beauty, she thought dismally. But at the age of twenty-three she had decided she was well and truly on the shelf enough to indulge in silk, and indulge she had. As a matter of fact, it was only the knowledge of four exceedingly elegant new dresses hanging in her closet that had persuaded her to acquiesce in this dismal weekend.

The sun-streaked chestnut hair was looped casually around her head, and the golden-brown eyes had a rueful expression. Given Lady Elfreda's overt enmity, Brenna's coolness, Sumner's self-absorption, and Adolphus's greedy paws, it was doubtless going to be a wretched time. The addition of the phenomenally stiff Sir Maurice and his villainous adjutant didn't sound much more promising. With a sigh and a longing thought toward dinner, she picked up her matching fan and moved with the air of a condemned prisoner to meet the rest of the houseparty.

So intent was she on her gloom and the distant scent of roast goose that she failed to notice that the previously deserted hall was no longer empty. Before she realized what she was doing, she collided full force with a broad male chest.

"I beg your pardon," she said breathlessly as she felt her arms gripped by iron fingers. A moment later she found herself ruthlessly put aside. Her arms were released, and she looked up into the face of what could only be the traitorous Michael Fraser.

Not quite Byronic, she thought absently, rubbing her bruised arms. He was taller than she, perhaps not quite as tall as her brother, though his shoulders in the austere black evening jacket were a great deal broader. He had dark brown, straight hair, dark blue eyes in a tanned, aloof face, high cheekbones, and a mouth that would have been alarmingly sensual had it not been for the grim line in which it was compressed. He stared down at Elizabeth for all the world as if she were an impertinent puppy.

"I'm sorry I ran into you," she said in her friendliest tones, smiling up at him. "I didn't expect anyone would be out here."

The smile that so often melted the hardest of hearts failed visibly to move this one, and he continued to stare down his well-shaped nose with cold hauteur. "My fault entirely," he said finally, completely without expression.

His voice was low-pitched and quite delightful, Elizabeth thought sadly. Spy or not, the man was a boor, just as she had suspected Sir Maurice's adjutant would be. Before she could make one last effort at civility, he moved away, disappearing into the room beside hers without a backward glance. The door shut firmly behind his tall, black figure, and Elizabeth uttered a short, sharp little word that would have horrified her proper brother.

"There you are, Elizabeth." Lady Elfreda greeted her in reproving tones when she finally reached the drawing room. "I had almost given you up. You never used to be so lamentably tardy. You remember my brother-in-law Maurice?"

There was nothing for the irritated Elizabeth to do but greet the aging soldier with a semblance of pleasure. Sir Maurice had never been a great favorite of hers. He was as short and stout as his sister-in-law was tall and thin, although they shared the same charm of manner and overwhelming family pride. He was also a desperate gamester and one of the hardest commanders the British Army had ever known. Adolphus was wont to boast of his uncle's excesses with a patronizing air, but the stories passed on to Elizabeth's unwilling ears from her brother Jeremy had given her a deep-seated horror of the man. As her eyes met his cruel little black ones, she could barely control a shudder of distaste.

"How pleasant to see you again, Miss Traherne. And looking lovelier than ever, I see. You do these old eyes good, I swear you do. Don't she, Dolph?" Sir Maurice's voice was curiously high-pitched and girlish, and unwillingly Elizabeth remembered the deep, slow tones of his secretary.

"I've told Elizabeth so many times," Adolphus said jovially, coming forth and taking one of her hands possessively. She resisted the impulse to slap him with her fan across the knuckles. "Let me make you known to my uncle's friend. The Contessa Leonora di Castello, late of the Peninsula. Contessa, this is Elizabeth Traherne."

Elizabeth found herself looking down at the most beautiful woman she had seen in her entire life. Jet black hair in an upsweep framed a heart-shaped face of pure white skin, with a tiny nose, dark, dark eyes, and a rosebud mouth that pouted fetchingly at all the gentlemen within her radius. The extremely low-cut black décolletage proclaimed her a widow, and a dashing one at that. Elizabeth could almost hear Adolphus salivating beside her, and she greeted the contessa with real enthusiasm.

The contessa smiled sleepily up at her, professing herself

delighted to meet another lovely young English lady. Those black eyes swept expressively toward Brenna's distant figure, and Elizabeth was amused to note the tiny pout on Brenna's lips. Sumner was as obviously fascinated by the contessa's lush charms as the other gentlemen, and Brenna hadn't expected to be eclipsed. If the Irish girl had ever been the slightest bit friendly, Elizabeth would have sympathized, but as it was she felt that Brenna was receiving her just deserts.

"And now where is Captain Fraser? This younger generation obviously fails to hold punctuality in the esteem we once did, eh, Maurice? Cook will be in despair," Lady Elfreda announced with a cheerful laugh. "You'll never keep him here at this rate, Dolph. He's threatened to leave you any time now."

"Pierre won't leave me until I'm ready to let him go," Adolphus said, unruffled, tearing his gaze away from the deep valley between the contessa's magnificent breasts. "And if I'm not mistaken, here is Captain Fraser."

Here he was indeed, Elizabeth thought. That same, grim, haughty figure entered the room, the dark blue eyes sweeping over the inhabitants like a commander reviewing the battlefield. From the speed with which that dark glance passed over her, she guessed that she rated somewhere between a broken cannon and a winded nag.

"Miss Traherne, allow me to introduce to you my uncle's current adjutant, Captain Michael Fraser, late of the Ninth Battalion. Fraser, this is my cousin, Miss Elizabeth Traherne. Fraser's been with Uncle Maurice for the past six months, and lucky you are to have him, eh, Uncle?"

The jovial tone in Adolphus's voice was at a strange variance with his earlier warnings, and Elizabeth stole a perplexed glance up at his bland, puffy face before nodding coolly at the unfriendly Captain Fraser. But Fraser's dark eyes, seemingly so uninterested in her charms, hadn't missed that quizzical expression, she realized with dismay, and he was watching Adolphus with a trace of the same curiosity, a bitter little smile lingering around his hard mouth.

Elizabeth was surprised to note that Lady Elfreda and she

shared the same low opinion of the chilly young man. "Well, since Captain Fraser has decided to rejoin us, perhaps we might go in to dinner before the goose is entirely ruined?" Again Lady Elfreda emitted that high-pitched laugh before she held out a commanding arm to her brother-in-law, an arm he dutifully accepted.

Goose, thought Elizabeth, her spirits brightening. She was so fond of goose, particularly stuffed with grapes. Her spirits dropped again when she realized who her dinner partner would be.

It went without saying that Adolphus would accompany the ranking female guest, the vibrant contessa, into the dining hall. Sumner could never be relegated to escorting his sister, and the look on Brenna O'Shea's face was that of a cat that had just swallowed a bowl of cream as she clasped Sumner's stalwart arm possessively. Fraser stood staring at her, the distant planes of his face unreadable in the flickering candlelight. Once more irritation rose within Elizabeth's breast.

She was used to hearing herself described as a very pretty young woman, one of the dashing Trahernes. She was therefore quite unused to a complete lack of reaction to her most charming wiles. As she looked up for a long, silent moment into Michael Fraser's dark, handsome face, pique combined with the memory of the baron's warning, and her worry over the absent Jeremy finished the job. The smile left her lips and eyes abruptly.

"Elizabeth!" Lady Elfreda's stentorian bellow echoed through the hall, and Elizabeth jumped nervously.

"You needn't accept my arm," Fraser said suddenly in that voice that had the uncanny knack of tickling Elizabeth's nerve endings. "I am not considered the most desirable dinner partner." The thought seemed to move him not one whit, and Elizabeth hardened herself to any latent sympathy.

"Well," she said brightly, taking his arm and following him out toward the immense dining hall, "if you *will* become a spy and a traitor, what would you expect? Though I would presume that being Sir Maurice's adjutant is punishment enough for any crime, no matter how treasonous." She waited calmly for the storm to erupt.

A strange sound emanated from the upright figure beside her, one that she might almost have suspected was a smothered laugh. But when she peeked up at him, the tanned face was as expressionless as before.

"I would suggest, Miss Traherne, that you not believe everything you hear. And that you certainly not repeat it."

"Oh, then you're not a spy?" She contrived to sound disappointed. "I was counting on you to liven up this rather dull weekend. I've never met a spy before." Except my own brother, she thought belatedly.

The muscles were iron hard beneath her hand, and for a moment Elizabeth regretted her rash tongue. "I have little doubt," he said after a long, tense moment, "that this weekend will be rather too lively. Even for a bored young social butterfly like yourself."

The censure was obvious in that deep voice, and the thought of her dutiful, active life as a whirl of social pleasures forced a chuckle from Elizabeth. "Then I will have to content myself to wait for the fireworks," she said cheerfully. "I am quite looking forward to it." She laughed again as she caught his sour glance down at her.

Chapter 4

DESPITE THE SUCCULENT goose stuffed with grapes, the grilled lake trout meunière, the Stilton soufflé, boiled mutton, and twelve vegetables, Elizabeth did not enjoy her dinner. Indeed, it was not to be wondered at, with a silent, disapproving dinner partner such as Michael Fraser on one side, an overly charming brother on the other, and a stern Lady Elfreda opposite watching her every move like a hawk. As a result, Elizabeth spilled soup on her new silk dress, choked on the goose, and ran out of forks far too soon.

There was nowhere she could turn for help. Adolphus's attention was firmly fixed on the contessa's remarkable cleavage; Sumner, above noticing such things, was nevertheless entranced by that lady's monosyllabic wit; and Brenna was struggling wildly to catch whatever dregs of Sumner's wandering attention might be available, her sharp green eyes daring Elizabeth to interfere. Elizabeth was never one to refuse a challenge, but in this case she felt not only unequal to the task of diverting Adolphus and Sumner but completely unwilling. If only the large, dark figure beside her were a little more lively, she could find it in her heart to be content.

She was halfway through a strawberry tart when she realized that all eyes were on her. Every plate was empty except hers, and every mouth was still as they patiently waited for her to finish her dessert. Swallowing in a suddenly dry throat, Elizabeth began to cough, choking into her damask napkin until her face turned scarlet and tears streamed from her eyes. Two smart thwacks between her vulnerable shoulder blades, much harder than was actually necessary, and she regained her composure.

"Thank you," she gasped to the silent captain, her brown eyes flashing her opinion of the force of his blows.

"Are you quite finished, Elizabeth?" Lady Elfreda questioned archly as she rose from her seat by Adolphus. "I am certain the gentlemen would appreciate some time to themselves. Adolphus, my pet, you must sec to raising Sumner's stipend. It would seem that they scarcely have enough to eat, though one wouldn't think so, looking at dear Elizabeth. Come along." And with that lightly spoken denunciation, Lady Elfreda swept from the room, a smirking Brenna in her wake, while the contessa, aided to her feet by three helpful pairs of hands, languidly followed.

Elizabeth's face was pink with embarrassment and the aftermath of her choking fit. Tossing her head back, she leaned over the table, snatched up two apples, and sauntered after the ladies, biting into one of them with deliberate grace. As she closed the door behind her, she heard a laugh, one that she failed to recognize, and wondered if Michael Fraser was human after all.

"Come sit by me, Miss Traherne." The contessa patted the silken sofa in an inviting gesture. "I would like to get to know you better. Our gracious hostess has dragged the little Irish girl off somewhere, so we can be comfortable for a few moments until the dragon returns, *hein*?"

Without hesitation Elizabeth offered the dazzling contessa one of her pilfered apples and plopped herself down beside her. "She is a bit of a tartar, isn't she?" she said cheerfully. "I dread having to come here, but Sumner *will* insist, and since it is only a few times a year, I suppose I can bear it for his sake."

"But why does she dislike you so much?" the lady questioned with great interest. "Me she hates because I am foreign, but you are the perfect young English lady. I would think you would be quite unexceptionable."

"Little do you know. Lady Elfreda is terrified that Adolphus means to make me his bride. I can't very well set her mind at rest by telling her I'd rather marry a dead slug, so instead I have to put up with her insults." Elizabeth took another bite of her apple, enjoying both the taste and the satisfying crunch.

"I wouldn't think it would be such a bad thing to be married to Sir Adolphus. After all, he is very rich, very important, and not bad looking if you do not mind a large man. One could do a great deal worse," she mused, pleating her black chiffon skirts thoughtfully.

Elizabeth watched her out of narrowed eyes, fascinated. "I wish you all the luck in the world, Contessa. You may have him with my blessing. That is . . . ," she stumbled, blushing.

The contessa let out an unaffected little trill of laughter. "You are obviously wondering what my relationship to Sir Maurice is but are much too polite to ask. You are wondering perhaps if I am his mistress, and what the old dragon would think if her brother-in-law's light-of-love married her son."

"No," said Elizabeth, but then her honesty took hold. "Well, actually, yes, I was wondering something of the sort. But I thought for once I might be discreet and watch my unruly tongue. Curiosity is one of my many flaws."

"Pooh. To be curious about other people is to be alive. I have no use for people who profess to have no interest in gossip. It is usually because they are only interested in themselves. I am afraid I cannot answer your unspoken question, however."

"But why not?" She finished the apple and contemplated a suitable repository for the core.

The contessa smiled a secret smile. "Because, my dear, you are that handsome clergyman's sister and a Christian young lady, and I can tell from your eyes that you would much rather not have to condemn me for my sins. So I shall spare you a recitation."

"Recitation?" Lady Elfreda strode back into the room, her olive skirts swirling behind her lanky figure. "Don't tell me you're some sort of play-actress, Contessa! My brother-in-law would surely have more sense than to bring that sort beneath my roof."

"Your brother-in-law, Lady Elfreda, is fully conscious of what he owes the name of Wingert," the contessa said smoothly. "Miss Traherne and I were discussing poets we have known, were we not?"

Thus adjured, Elizabeth nodded solemnly. "Where is

Brenna?" she questioned, not from any real interest but to change a somewhat dangerous subject.

Lady Elfreda gave her the customary smile of cold disapproval. "Off seeing to her duties. We're expecting another friend of Maurice's tomorrow. I doubt you're acquainted with Sir Henry and Lady Beatrice Hatchett; they don't precisely move in your limited circles." She gave a heavy sigh. "I'm afraid I cannot even trust the maids nowadays without someone standing over them all the time. Brenna does admirably. So suited in every way to be chatelaine of a large estate."

"Well, when Adolphus gets married, perhaps Brenna might find a job as a housekeeper somewhere," Elizabeth said sweetly, dropping her apple core on the coffee tray in front of her. "It is so useful to have a trade."

"Winfields is such a lovely place," the contessa interrupted hastily. "You must be very proud."

Her ladyship's lizard-like eyes glimmered faintly at the blatant flattery, and with a great show she turned her narrow, ramrod-straight back on her obstreperous guest, smiling graciously at the no longer despised contessa.

"I am indeed, dear Contessa. Wingerts have been in residence here since the thirteenth century, and Wingerts have served the Crown in various capacities down through the years. My brother-in-law Maurice is merely the latest in a long line of proud and loyal Wingerts devoted to their king and country." She allowed herself a glare in Elizabeth's direction. "Wingerts have always been soldiers and statesmen," she added proudly.

"Rather than clerics and artists," that damsel spoke up unadvisedly. "I had noticed a somewhat bellicose attitude in your ladyship. It must run in the blood."

Lady Elfreda's strong jaw snapped shut, and she rose to her full height, towering over the uncowed Elizabeth. Before she could order the unrepentant girl from the room, however, the miscreant rose with a great yawn.

"I believe I'll retire and not wait for the gentlemen, difficult as it is for me to tear myself away from such company," she announced with a limpid smile. "If you'll make my excuses to

Adolphus and Sir Maurice?"

"And what about poor Michael?" the contessa asked suddenly, with a sly smile that made Elizabeth momentarily quite uncomfortable. "Don't you wish us to make your excuses to him?"

"Certainly," Elizabeth said coolly, with a betraying flush. Before Lady Elfreda could unburden herself of the harangue bubbling just beneath her armor-like surface, she was off. As she closed the door, she heard Lady Elfreda's snort of outrage.

"Unprincipled baggage!" that lady announced. Strain as she might, Elizabeth couldn't quite hear the contessa's muffled reply.

The sounds of boisterous male laughter carried down the hall from the dining room, and Elizabeth breathed a small sigh of relief. The last thing she wanted to do was run into any of the four gentlemen now well into their port and cigars. Most of all she wished to avoid Adolphus with the greedy hands, though the surly Michael Fraser ranked a close second. Never had she met a man more ill-bred, cold-blooded, unfriendly... and quite handsome, she found herself adding with her customary honesty. What a shame such attractive looks were wasted on such a villain. She mustn't forget that he was Jeremy's enemy and therefore her own.

She passed Brenna in the upper hall, and the Irish girl met her expression incuriously. "Retiring so soon?" she questioned with the slight Irish burr Sumner doubtless found so attractive. "The gentlemen will be desolate."

Having vented her spleen recently, Elizabeth met Brenna's catty remark with a calm smile. "I doubt they'll even notice. I'm afraid I didn't leave Lady Elfreda in too charitable a temper."

Brenna grimaced, tossing back her midnight curls with a gesture Elizabeth wished she could duplicate. "That would be nothing new. You're having more company at your end of the hall. I've put Sir Henry and Lady Beatrice on the other side of your room. At least they'll be able to protect you from Michael Fraser if he proves to be as bad as he's suspected."

"Is he a villain?" Elizabeth questioned, and Brenna shrugged her slender shoulders.

"I really have no idea, nor do I care. The man is hardly my type. Nor, should I think, would he be yours, Elizabeth."

"And what do you suppose is my type?" Elizabeth asked with great interest. "I have yet to discover it myself."

"I cannot imagine. But I wouldn't think it would be a dangerously attractive rogue such as Michael Fraser. Good night, Elizabeth." Before she could reply, Brenna had sailed off down the hall, leaving Elizabeth chuckling softly.

Not for one moment had she failed to interpret Brenna's motives. There was nothing more likely to excite a woman's romantic imagination than to call a man a dangerously attractive rogue. And he was that, Elizabeth had to admit. Curse Brenna's facile tongue. No doubt she'd dream of the creature tonight. It was only fortunate that he was so obviously ineligible; otherwise, she might be bothered by his cold lack of interest in her.

Once she reached the vast confines of her room, however, Elizabeth was not the slightest bit tired. A good fire was blazing in the marble hearth, the massive four-poster bed was turned down, and beside the bed on the papier-mâché table was Elizabeth's newest French novel and a tin of comfits thoughtfully provided by the reliable Mrs. Gibson. Elizabeth gave a sigh of pure pleasure and prepared to abandon herself to sin.

She was well into the third chapter of *Le Cri d'amour* when her stays began to dig into her tender flesh. The house was quiet except for the muffled bumps of the maid as she prepared the Hatchetts' room for their arrival tomorrow. The one problem with her new silk dresses, Elizabeth thought as she scrambled off the bed, was that she required help in undoing the thirty-odd buttons that trailed down her backbone. She usually preferred to do without the ministrations of a maid, but after fifteen minutes of struggling behind her back, she gave up. The dress was undone halfway down and falling off her shoulders, but despite the most absurd contortions she couldn't reach the remaining buttons.

Hampering the situation was the fact that she had taken down her thick chestnut hair, and the waist-length locks were tangling with the buttons. She would have to ring for a maid; there was no help for it. From bitter experience Elizabeth knew just how unhelpful and elusive Lady Elfreda's servants could be. They obviously modeled their behavior after that of their ungracious mistress. Sighing, she rang the bell and then sat down to wait.

Four rings and twenty minutes later, Elizabeth gave up. The knocks and bumps still emanated from the bedroom next to hers. There was nothing she could do but quietly seek the aid of the chambermaid next door and trust that no one would catch her in her deshabille. Her reputation was undeservedly shaky as it was, and to be caught wandering around Winfields half naked would have put her beyond the pale.

Tiptoeing across the room on stocking feet, she listened for a long nervous moment. There still was no sound but the cautious bumping of the maid. She slipped out into the deserted hallways and whisked into the Hatchetts' room.

"I wonder if you could help me undo my dress."

The words faltered on her tongue. The shadowed figure turned and moved into the light. Staring down at her was Michael Fraser, his coat gone, his shirt open, and his dark hair awry. A handsome devil indeed, Elizabeth thought, as a wave of embarrassment washed over her.

"I beg your pardon," she breathed, her face flushed as she tried to pull the slipping gown around her. "I thought you were the maid."

"Obviously I am not."

Struggling to regain her composure, she cast a harried glance about her. There was no sign of his possessions anywhere. "I thought this was the Hatchetts' room."

"It is."

Elizabeth was startled by the bald statement. "I suppose Sir Maurice asked you to check and make sure everything was in order for their arrival," she said, offering him an excuse for his odd presence in the empty room, momentarily forgetting her own precarious situation.

"You could suppose so, but he didn't. I'm here on my own."

"Why?"

"I have no intention of satisfying that formidable curiosity, Miss Traherne," he replied calmly, moving across the room with a panther's grace. "I believe you wished your gown undone?"

There was a gleam in those dark blue eyes, and Elizabeth began to back away hastily. She took no more than two steps, when he caught her, his cool, impersonal hands holding her prisoner and making her uncomfortably aware of just how helpless she was. The heavy curtain of hair was moved gently out of the way, and she felt his hands deftly undo the recalcitrant buttons. A moment later the dress was loose, the hands released her, and she jumped away as if burned.

Very dangerously attractive, she thought absently, staring up at that dark face for a long, breathless minute. "I . . . thank you," she stammered, and was surprised to see a small smile quirk his mouth.

"My pleasure, Miss Traherne." The low voice was curiously caressing. "Any time."

For once Elizabeth's facile wit deserted her. The cold daylight with her clothes safely about her was one matter, but alone in a bedroom with her dress slipping down her shoulders and her hair unbound and Michael Fraser looking at her out of those unfathomable blue eyes—that was a different story. A rogue indeed, and certainly more than she was used to handling. She knew she should run away, back to the safety of her room.

"Should you be in here?" she questioned.

"Should you?"

She ignored that. "What would Adolphus and Sir Maurice say?"

"You could always tell them and find out," he suggested amiably.

"No, I don't think I'll do that."

Interest lit his dark face. "Why not, pray tell?"

An impish grin flitted across her expressive features. "Because, my dear Captain Fraser, if you really happen to be a spy and a traitor, then I intend to be the one to catch you red-handed. I see no reason to let the men have all the fun and excitement."

The small smile vanished from his face. "Do you have any

idea how dangerous that notion is?" he demanded harshly. "Spying doesn't happen to be a parlor game."

"I bow to your superior knowledge," she said demurely. "Are you a spy?" This was sounding unexpectedly close to a confession.

"Don't be absurd. You've been reading too many French novels."

Elizabeth looked at him with swift suspicion. If he could gain entry to the Hatchetts' room, there was no reason why he should not have searched hers as well. The mention of the French novels was a bit too fortuitous. But what in the world would he expect to find in the bedroom of a vicar's sister? Or was it her other brother who interested him—the British soldier involved on a secret mission?

"How did you know I read French novels?" she questioned sharply.

"You look the type," he said in a blunt voice. "Go to bed, Miss Traherne. This is hardly the time or place to be holding a tête-à-tête on espionage."

With great dignity Elizabeth wrapped the falling dress more securely around her. "I don't need you to tell me correct behavior, sir," she said proudly.

"No? You don't seem to pay any heed to your clerical brother. Are you going to bed, Miss Traherne, or will I have to take you there?"

There was a silken threat in his voice, and Elizabeth judged it time to depart. She only wished she could think of something cold and withering to leave on, but her usually quick brain failed her.

"Good evening, Captain Fraser," she snapped, and swept from the room, giving the door a solid little slam behind her. Once inside her own chamber she propped a chair under the gilt doorknob to prevent unwanted visitors and then threw herself down in front of the mirrored dressing table.

Her golden-brown eyes were wide and shining, her cheeks flushed, her lips breathlessly parted, with the tousled curtain of hair sweeping her pretty white shoulders. "If this is what the type of person who reads French novels looks like," she remarked aloud, "then I should cultivate the habit even more assiduously."

Then, humming a cheerful little tune, she stripped off the rest of her clothing and crawled wearily between the heavy linen sheets. She shut her eyes and then opened them again as his words returned with sudden, ominous meaning.

"Your clerical brother," he had said, his tone suggesting that he knew full well she had another, less conventionally employed sibling. If he knew about Jeremy and his covert activities, he was dangerous indeed. A sudden thrill of fear shot through Elizabeth's stomach, and she thrashed restlessly in the bed, punching the soft feather pillows, determined to keep her ears open for any more compromising noises from Captain Fraser. A moment later she was sound asleep.

Chapter 5

"WHAT WERE YOU doing for such a long time?" The dulcet voice drifted to Michael's ears as he silently let himself back into his room. Whirling around, he saw the contessa's languid black-draped figure stretched out on the damask-covered bed. He shut the door noiselessly behind himself and moved into his room.

"What do you think I was doing?" he countered mildly. "And do you think you should be in here? What if somebody saw you?"

The contessa's ruby lips pouted prettily. "I am offended, my dear Michael. You of all people should know that I'm an old enough hand to be able to sneak in and out of bedrooms without anyone being the wiser. And there's hardly anyone in this rambling mausoleum worthy of my talents. I'm certain everyone else is sound asleep, snoring mightily."

"Including Sir Maurice?" he asked cynically.

"Oh, I made certain dear Maurice was dead to the world before I started on my nocturnal perambulations. He won't be bothering me any more tonight." She smiled lazily.

"You know, Leonora," Michael said casually as he stretched himself out on a chair quite a ways from the comfortable bed and its enticing occupant, "there are times you are so efficient you frighten me. What else have you accomplished in between drugging Sir Maurice insensate and sneaking into my bedroom?"

"Did I say I drugged Sir Maurice?" she purred. "There are other ways of making an elderly gentleman sleep the sleep of the dead." She patted the coverlet invitingly.

"I am sure there are." Michael ignored the gesture, and Leonora shrugged her pretty white shoulders philosophically.

"I did happen to overhear the most enlightening conversation," she offered slowly, and his attention was immediate. "I was completely amazed."

"Was it with—"

"It was between the young English lady and a certain gentleman of somewhat tarnished reputation behind a closed bedroom door. I swear, I was all agog when he offered to take the chit to bed. Especially when he's refused so many other offers."

For a moment the expression in those dark blue eyes was dangerous. Then he smiled. "You will learn, Leonora, to mind your own business."

"I doubt it. At this point in my life my business *is* other people's secrets." She leaned back and sighed. "It would be so nice to retire from our questionable profession, Michael. I rather fancy our distinguished host. Don't you think I might make an excellent baroness?"

"Without question. You might run into a bit of opposition from Lady Elfreda, however. I'd be more frightened of her than anyone you've met with in your varied career."

"I could handle her," Leonora said with a confident toss of her elegantly tousled coiffure. "However, that's not to say that I wouldn't prefer throwing in my lot with you, dear boy. I'd be willing to put up with a great deal of . . . shall we say uncertainty . . . for the sake of those beautiful blue eyes."

"I am more than flattered, Leonora. But you know as well as I that we simply wouldn't suit. You'd be off with someone a great deal richer and a great deal less demanding than I would be, leaving me and the children bereft."

"The children?" she questioned, and shuddered. "Perhaps you're right, dear boy. Ours is a love that will never be."

"You wasted your talents, Leonora. You should have been on the stage."

"Don't be absurd. My acting talent is put to much better use in my present field, and I make a very great deal more money than I ever would in Drury Lane. I have no regrets."

Michael shifted, in the chair, his deep blue eyes narrowed in the dim light from the banked fire and his long, lean legs stretched out in front of him. "Apart from having no regrets, would it be too bold of me to inquire whether you have any pertinent information to impart? Or did you just make this foray to eavesdrop on Elizabeth Traherne?"

"No information as yet," she said pertly. "Which I thought you might like to know. Also, I came for the sake of those blue eyes. I am getting very tired of Sir Maurice."

"No doubt you are. You might remember that Adolphus Wingert's eyes are also blue. It shouldn't be too much longer now. Surely you can hold out a few more days."

"I suppose so," she replied with a sigh, rising with leisurely grace from the bed. "So Miss Traherne's name is Elizabeth. I wonder that you should commit it to memory."

There was no expression on the tanned, handsome face. "Wonder away," he said affably.

"She's a nice girl. Far too lively for this crowd and far too nice for a conscienceless rogue like you, Michael Fraser."

"If you had put that pretty shell-pink ear a little closer to the door, you would have heard me trying to get rid of her," he said mildly.

"I heard enough. You forget I've known you for at least five years. You may be able to fool yourself, but you aren't about to fool me."

Michael rose to his full six feet two. "You know, Leonora, I think you're quite right. It is past time you retired. You're beginning to become prey to the most alarming fancies. I should warn you, however. It wouldn't do to underestimate friend Adolphus. I have the vague suspicion he's not the amiable buffoon he appears to be."

"You don't think he's involved?" she said sharply, suddenly all business.

"I haven't made up my mind yet. He could bear some watching, however. I get the impression there's a great deal more brain behind that somewhat asinine expression."

Leonora smiled sweetly. "And it would behoove you to take Miss Traherne a bit more seriously. Sumner Traherne may be a charming idiot, but that girl has a head on her shoulders."

Michael nodded. "I'll do my best to avoid her."

"That might be the wisest course. It would be extremely unfortunate if she were to stick that well-shaped nose of hers someplace where it didn't belong. Were she to come across the wrong sort of information, drastic steps would be taken, Michael."

"Leave the drastic steps to me, my dear contessa." His voice slid ironically around her title. "You have enough of your own to keep you busy." He took her slender, silk-clad arm in one hand and led her gently, inexorably to the door.

She accepted her *congé* with good grace. Looking up at him out of thickly lashed eyes, she sighed soulfully. "I could wish this were all over with."

"It will be soon enough," he said with a noticeable lack of sympathy, giving her a gentle shove through the door. "In the meantime try to be a bit more circumspect. I don't have quite as much faith as you have in your powers of dissimulation."

"You're a sweet boy," she said impishly, reaching up and kissing him swiftly on one lean cheek.

The door closed behind her, and she moved swiftly down the hallway on silent feet. But despite Fraser's doubts, she was fully aware of the silent closing of the door at the end of the hall, and she uttered a silent curse beneath her breath. First thing tomorrow she must find out who was stationed in that distant bedroom and who would have seen her kissing Sir Maurice's handsome adjutant somewhere past midnight in the door of his bedroom. He was right; she was getting far too slipshod. Thank heavens it was almost over.

Chapter 6

Saturday

ELIZABETH AWOKE as usual shortly after dawn. It took her a moment or two to remember where she was in the first light, and she squinted around the lofty proportions of her bedchamber with a curious sense of anticipation. The source of that excitement escaped her memory as she climbed out of bed and dashed across the icy floor to the meager warmth of the banked fire. Then she looked at the wall and remembered the room beyond with its infuriating and mysterious occupant.

She dressed swiftly in a warm wool dress of dark blue with few enough buttons to allow her to manage on her own. Arranging her chestnut hair in attractive, loose coils, she went off in search of coffee, her slippered feet silent in the empty halls.

It was too early for breakfast to be set up, and so with an unerring instinct and her excellent sense of smell Elizabeth found her way to the busy basement kitchen, where fresh-brewed coffee and an assortment of cinnamon buns still warm from the oven awaited her. The temperamental French chef who was Adolphus's pride and joy was still sleeping the sleep of the just, and in his place was the warm, comfortable figure of Mrs. Kingpin, whose greatest joy was to feed a hungry young lady.

"It's a treat to see you again, Miss Elizabeth," she said fondly. "I was telling that Moosewer Peeyair that we don't see enough of you here at Winfields."

"Don't be getting any ideas, Mrs. Kingpin. I have no intention of taking up residence," Elizabeth said hastily, reaching for a cinnamon bun.

The older woman's flushed face crinkled in disappointment. "Then there's to be no match between you and Sir Adolphus?"

"No match. Can you imagine what his mother would say?" she questioned with a trace of mischief.

"I can indeed. But we at Winfields have learned that it's Sir Adolphus who has the final say when it all comes down to brass tacks. Lady Elfreda can fuss and fume all she wants; Sir Adolphus gets his way."

"He has more than Lady Elfreda to contend with this time," Elizabeth replied, taking a deep drink of the hot, rich coffee. Sumner considered it unpatriotic not to drink tea, but Elizabeth had a passion for the strong brew that was Mrs. Kingpin's specialty. "I have no desire for the match, either. Why wouldn't Brenna do?"

Mrs. Kingpin shook her head. "He won't have any part of her. She's not a bad girl, either, though with that temper of hers and her headstrong ways she might have a bit of trouble. But she'll make someone a fine wife." Mrs. Kingpin's face was deliberately bland.

"Someone like my brother Sumner?" Elizabeth questioned calmly.

"There has been some mention of that possibility," the cook admitted. "She's very good at managing a house, Miss Elizabeth, and she's got a nice touch with the staff. The vicar could do a lot worse."

"You don't have to convince me. It's Sumner who'll do the deciding. As far as I'm concerned, she has my blessing." She drained the thick kitchen mug and held it out for more. "Tell me, Mrs. Kingpin, do you know anything about Michael Fraser?"

"Is that the young gentleman with Sir Maurice? This is the first time he's been here. I gather he's under a bit of a cloud, but he seems like a nice enough gentleman. Has a lovely smile, he does."

"A smile?" Elizabeth echoed.

"And beautiful manners. Always a kind word for the staff. Why, no one minded his questions in the least, so courteous he was in his manner of asking."

"Questions?" Elizabeth's ears pricked up. "What sort of questions?"

"Oh, nothing terribly exciting. He wanted to know about the various entrances and exits to Winfields and whether there'd been any strangers about, and was there any spot a person could hide where he wouldn't be discovered. I presume it had to do with Sir Maurice. We were as helpful as we could be, Miss Elizabeth."

"I'm sure you were," she said grimly.

"He was particularly interested in you, Miss Elizabeth, if you don't mind my saying so. Wanted to know all about that poor drowned Frenchy you found and whether it was a habit of yours to go wandering down by the ocean alone. It seems to me, miss, that he's fair taken with you. Happen he might have an accidental assignation in mind."

Elizabeth's palms were damp with sudden panic. The thought of that cool, aloof soldier asking about her failed to fill her with conceit. He might very well have something outwardly accidental in mind, but she doubted it was a romantic assignation such as Mrs. Kingpin imagined. She cleared her dry throat nervously. "Perhaps" was all she vouchsafed. "What did he want to know about the French sailor?"

"Oh, whether anyone else was seen around the body, whether a ship was seen in the vicinity, that sort of thing." Mrs. Kingpin shrugged. "He also asked whether anyone thought the sailor's death might have been something more than an accident." She shook her graying head. "Such a morbid streak for such a nice young man."

"And what did you tell him?" Elizabeth asked casually, sipping her coffee.

"Why, the truth, of course. That there was nothing the slightest bit suspicious about the entire thing. He was just some poor sailor washed overboard during a storm. Unpleasant for you to have to find him, but you've got plenty of pluck, miss, and so I told him: 'Miss Elizabeth wouldn't be the sort to go all faint at the sight of a dead man. If there'd been anyone around, she would have seen him.' That's what I told him. And didn't Sir

Adolphus himself hold an inquiry, as is his duty as justice of the peace, and declare that everything was as it seemed?"

"Of course." Elizabeth agreed faintly, remembering only too well. She remembered Adolphus's absolute refusal to hear her observations on the matter, blandly ignoring any conflicting evidence, such as the disparity between the rough seaman's clothing and the white, fine-boned hands that had never known a day's hard labor. It was no ordinary sailor Elizabeth had found washed up on the beach at Starfield Cove, his neck at an ominous angle. But no one would listen to her conjectures, and she eventually gave up, missing Jeremy more than ever. He, at least, would have listened to her. Adolphus's belated doubts, confided to her last evening, were too little, too late.

"You don't seem to care for Captain Fraser, miss. He seemed like a very charming gentleman to me," Mrs. Kingpin offered hesitantly.

"Are we talking about the same man?" Elizabeth mused. "The Michael Fraser I met was cold, grim, and rude. I don't think he even knows how to smile." Except in that odiously disturbing way as she stood in front of him with her dress falling off, she amended silently.

"Maybe you went about it in the wrong way. I can't imagine a gentleman being immune to your charms, Miss Elizabeth. If you'd just smile up at him, I have no doubt he'll respond."

"I've tried it several times, Mrs. Kingpin. For some reason he seems to have taken me in dislike."

"Well, it could be that you remind him of his past. He might well have a broken heart; I've heard of such things." Mrs. Kingpin sighed sentimentally and dabbed at an eye with the corner of her capacious apron. "That can often explain a gentleman's moodiness."

"Who has a broken heart?" Brenna's bright voice broke in. "Not Elizabeth, I trust?" There was a malicious gleam in her large green eyes.

"Not I, Brenna. I have a heart of flint; ask anyone. We were discussing the mysterious Captain Fraser. Mrs. Kingpin will have it that I might resemble one of his lost loves."

"I doubt it," Brenna said shortly, taking the seat at the scrubbed kitchen table that Mrs. Kingpin had deserted and accepting a cup of tea.

"How very flattering you are," Elizabeth said in dulcet tones when the kitchen helpers were out of hearing.

"I would have thought you'd prefer to know where I stand," she replied in a sharp voice.

"I would love to know where you stand. I'm afraid I haven't quite figured it out yet. If it's my brother's hand and heart you're interested in, I must tell you that you have my blessing."

"You'll have to give me leave to doubt that," Brenna said cynically.

"Why in the world should you? There is nothing I would like better than to be released from my sisterly duties. I've always expected him to marry sooner or later, and you seem as good a candidate as any. Provided you care just a tiny bit for him."

"I love him!" Brenna shot back, and Elizabeth had no reason to doubt the vehemence of the claim.

"But for heaven's sake why?" she questioned curiously. "He's very handsome, of course, but not clever or terribly wealthy. As a matter of fact, he's a charming, pompous bore with the saving grace of having a kind heart. Why should you be in love with him?"

"I happen to consider a kind heart rather a high priority," Brenna said with great dignity. "And you needn't insult him to try and convince me that you aren't monstrously possessive. Sumner has told me how you've determined to devote your life to him. I suppose when a woman fails to find a husband, there's nothing else for her to do but try to smother the only other men in her life with mindless devotion It's really rather touching, but I will have to tell you, Elizabeth, that he doesn't need it. Not with me by his side. You can devote yourself to your brother Jeremy when he returns."

Elizabeth took a deep, calming breath, controlling her temper and saving it for her conceited idiot brother. "Are you by his side?" she inquired mildly. "Has he made you an offer?"

"He is about to," Brenna shot back.

Elizabeth hesitated for only a moment and then put her hand on Brenna's tightly clenched one. "I mean it, Brenna. You have my blessing. And you needn't worry that I'd continue to live with you. If Jeremy doesn't need me, I thought of setting up house on my own with my old governess for a companion. Your marriage would give me the excuse I've always needed."

"Sumner will never let you," Brenna said warily.

"Despite what folderol Sumner might have told you, *I* control my money and my life, not him. I would like us to be friends, Brenna." Warm brown eyes looked into angry green ones for a long moment. "And I will be delighted to dance at your wedding."

A hesitant smile curved Brenna's mouth. "All right. I wouldn't be minding dancing at my own wedding one bit. If we can just keep that harridan at bay. Sumner could barely keep his eyes off the great vulgar creature."

"The contessa? Sumner?" Elizabeth laughed. "I wouldn't worry if I were you. If Sumner is fool enough to prefer her to you, then he wasn't worth the bother in the first place."

"That's easy for you to say."

"I suppose it is. But I know my brother well enough to know that any foolishness on his part will be short-lived. He has a remarkable capacity for self-protection, and he'll know well enough where his future comfort will lie. In the meantime I'll do my best to keep them apart, but you'll have to take it from there. I shouldn't doubt you'll be able to bring him up to scratch before we leave here."

"You'd do that for me?" Brenna breathed.

"For you and for Sumner. And for myself, too."

Her hand paused over another cinnamon bun. Her mind went back to Michael Fraser, and she restrained herself, holding out her hand to Brenna instead. After a final moment's hesitation, the Irish girl shook it, smiling up at her future sister-in-law uncertainly.

"And if you ever need any help, Elizabeth . . ."

"I will let you know. And it may be sooner than you think."

Chapter 7

THERE WAS A STIFF breeze blowing that morning, tossing the newly budded branches wildly overhead and drying the dew-spangled grounds until the flagstones and the beckoning grasses glistened in the bright sunlight. As Elizabeth stared out the library windows, she had little doubt that it would be hours before the others arose from their slothful beds, and glad she was of it. There wasn't a single member of this oddly assorted houseparty with whom she cared to spend more time, with the possible exception of the mysterious and charming contessa. As for Michael Fraser, he could sleep till doomsday for all she cared. And probably would, she thought impatiently, wrapping the black silk shawl closer around her and opening the French door. The wind tried to snap it shut in her face, but Elizabeth was nothing if not determined. With a fierce word and a yank she opened it again and slipped out into the windy sunshine.

It was not precisely the weather or the circumstances for a casual walk. Ladies usually strolled the afternoon, accompanied by a maid, a footman, or several other ladies of similar tastes, with parasols over their heads to shade them from the sun and not a breath of wind in the sky. Elizabeth wrapped the black shawl around her head to keep the stiff breeze from yanking her chestnut hair out of its loose pinnings and strode determinedly onward, head down into the wind, her dark blue skirts swirling around her long legs.

"Contessa!" a voice hissed from the underbrush. Elizabeth halted her headlong pace, staring about her. She was at the edge of the second terraced lawn, and at this hour not a soul was in sight. The noise came again, the hissed sibilants sounding not unlike her own name.

"Yes?" she replied uncertainly, peering through the boxwood thicket. "Who is it?" She had unconsciously lowered her voice to a hoarse whisper.

"Who the 'ell do you think it is?" the voice came back irritably as a short, crafty-looking man in moleskin trousers and greasy weskit rose up out of the underbrush. "Who else would yer worship be expecting at an hour past daybreak in this 'ere bleedin' garden? I thought you weren't coming."

Elizabeth stared, fascinated. "But I'm not who you—" She broke it off, cursing her own ready honesty.

She had nothing to worry about. The small man let out a short bark of laughter "Oh, you're not, are you? And why else would a lady of the house, dressed in black, be taking a walk at seven-thirty in the morning on such a windy day if not to meet with Wat Simpkin, may I ask?" he snorted. "I don't blame ye for being careful, Contessa, but I ain't got time to waste."

Elizabeth did her best to look knowledgeable. "Of course," she murmured, pulling the shawl more closely about her.

"First of all, I've got a message for himself from Mr. Fredericks. He's to come down to Starfield Cove this afternoon if he doesn't want certain people to find out what happened there last month."

"What did happen?" Elizabeth found herself asking.

Wat Simpkin's begrimed face creased in an expression of exasperation, and he spat. "Don't come all innocent with me, yer worship. You know as well as I that spying, conniving LeBoeuf met his untimely end down there. Helped along by a mutual acquaintance of ours. Fredericks don't want anyone getting wind of that spot of helpfulness, so he says for me to tell you to send 'is nibs down there, and we'll see what we can do. Any luck finding the paper?"

"I beg your pardon?"

"Listen, Contessa." Mr. Simpkin edged closer to Elizabeth, who uneasily stood her ground. "You're here at Winfields to find the list of English agents LeBoeuf hid before anyone else does. Not to have a good time. Didn't our friend explain it to you?"

"Well, he didn't really have much time," Elizabeth said vaguely.

"Was there ever such an ill-managed piece of work?" Wat demanded of the cloudless sky, which forbore to answer him. He turned back to the false contessa. "Haven't ye wondered why ye should be coming down at this unlikely time, in the beginning of the London season and all?"

"Well, yes, I did."

"And he didn't tell you we need that paper before anyone else finds it?" he demanded patiently. "The list of English agents active in France right now. You can imagine how they'd like to get hold of that. They'd pay a pretty penny for that sort of information."

"I suppose they would. Where is it?"

"That's the problem, missus. No one knew but LeBoeuf, and I'm afraid he died before he had the chance to tell. And maybe the man that LeBoeuf came here to meet, whoever he is. No one tells me anything, but Mr. Fredericks says the government has a good idea who he is, and they're planning on catching him in the act when he finds the papers. Of course, we have to find where the papers are first. Those papers are worth their weight in gold, and who's to know if we sell them to the highest bidder? Certainly not Fredericks."

Elizabeth hesitated. "It sounds attractive."

"I knew ye were a downy one the moment I laid eyes on ye," said Wat, spitting for emphasis.

"Does the man know they suspect him?" she inquired, wondering who "he" was and hoping oddly that it wasn't Michael Fraser.

"Don't think so. Sir Henry here yet?"

"He's due by teatime," Elizabeth replied vaguely, her mind turning cartwheels.

"Keep an eye out for him. And tell himself to be very careful. The man's got eyes in his head."

"You mean—"

"No names," he interrupted, peering about him. "You never know who might overhear. We can both guess who it is they're suspecting."

No, we can't, Elizabeth wailed inwardly. "But what should I do?"

"Keep looking for that paper. We need to find it before the traitor does. Failing that, keep your eyes peeled and do nothing. Just tell our friend what I've told you. Sir Henry is determined to catch the traitor with the information in hand this time. Tell him that I'll be down at Starfield Cove as we arranged, and Fredericks will be with me. If he still wants to talk with us, we'll be waiting. Otherwise, it's in his hands, and I wish him all the luck."

"But who . . ."

The gentleman in the moleskin trousers disappeared back into the underbrush. Elizabeth beat about ineffectually, but the gnome-like creature had vanished.

"Damn," she said, enjoying the sound of the word out where no one could hear her. If she ever gained her freedom from Sumner, she'd make it a practice to swear out loud every chance she got.

Wat Simpkin was nowhere in sight, and Elizabeth cursed again in frustration. All this talk of "our friend" and "himself" and "he" and "traitors" and "agents," and she had no way of sorting through Wat Simpkin's garbled message and knowing who played which role. Of only one thing could she be certain. There was a highly dangerous list of English agents hidden somewhere in this moldering old place, a list that might very well contain her brother Jeremy's name. If the traitor found it before the combined forces representing the British government did, his life might very well be forfeit.

Sir Henry was coming to catch the traitor red-handed. The contessa's role in all this was highly suspect, and heaven only knew who the traitor might be. Fraser was the logical choice, but something inside Elizabeth rebelled at the thought. There was only one thing she could do: make her way down to Starfield Cove this afternoon and see what she could see. Presuming that the mysterious Mr. Fredericks worked for the British government and not the French, presuming that the message intended for the contessa somehow reached "himself," presuming that she could somehow make some sense of this tangled mess.

But whether she liked it or not, things didn't look good for the grim and silent Captain Fraser, who was already far too curious about the dead sailor. Chances were, it was those well-shaped hands that had precipitated poor LeBoeuf's departure, though with what purpose Elizabeth couldn't guess. She shuddered at the memory, less endowed with pluck than Mrs. Kingpin supposed.

Her pace back to the house was a great deal slower, even with the wind at her back. What she should do, of course, would be to confront Sir Henry when he arrived and tell him everything she knew. And she might very well do just that. But not right away, she thought. She could at least give Michael Fraser time to prove himself. Couldn't she?

In the meantime she would use her time to good advantage and do her best to find that incriminating list of spies herself. After all, she was fully as bright as the devious contessa and, because of her almost-cousinship with Adolphus, far more familiar with Winfields and its environs. No one would think she had any knowledge that such an incriminating list existed, much less that she would be after it for herself.

It came as no surprise to her to see the contessa's black-clad figure on the terrace, watching her approach out of hooded eyes. "What a strange time for a walk, Miss Traherne," she said in silken tones. "I wouldn't have thought you would be out of bed so early, much less tramping around in the fields."

"Oh, I'm an early riser. I always enjoy going for a walk before anyone but the servants are up. You look as if you enjoy doing the same," she added, with a pointed look at the light pelisse and heavy veiling ready to be placed around the contessa's distinctive features.

Much to Elizabeth's respectful surprise, the contessa laughed lightly and unaffectedly, the warm chuckle in her throat a delightful sound on the morning air. "As a matter of fact, I confess I was about to do exactly that. I don't need much sleep. I retire late and rise early. Would you care to accompany me, Miss Traherne?"

Elizabeth mentally bowed before the more experienced schemer. "I've had enough for the time being, thank you. But I'm certain you'll enjoy yourself. Not a soul in sight, not even the gardeners. It's delightfully peaceful." With a nod and a smile, she passed the contessa and went back into the house. Had she looked back, she would have seen a speculative expression on the contessa's pale but beautiful face, and she would have felt less smug.

"THERE YOU ARE, my little pigeon!" Sir Adolphus greeted Elizabeth cheerfully from behind a mountain of food. "I thought you were still abed. How delightful that we should have such a beautiful companion to our bachelor breakfast, eh what, gentlemen?"

Sumner, equally engrossed in a positively gluttonous breakfast, responded with a muffled "*mmphh*." Michael Fraser looked at her steadily out of dark blue eyes, and Elizabeth stared right back, trying to see behind that politely distant face to the possible villainy beneath it.

"Miss Traherne is an addition to any situation, no matter how unusual," he said at last. His eyes were speaking of last night, and only by sheer force of will did Elizabeth keep from blushing.

"Hear, hear. Fraser, I would hardly call breakfast at Winfields an unusual situation," Adolphus said indulgently. "Why, I have it all the time. Pay no attention to young Fraser, Elizabeth. He's trying to turn your head with his odd sort of flattery. Does that work on the Continent, my boy? Our English girls aren't quite used to it, don't you know."

A brief, cold smile lit Fraser's dark face. "Oh, I have other ways of flirtation, Sir Adolphus. I'll be glad to give Miss Traherne a demonstration some time when we're alone."

Sumner choked on his cinnamon bun and glared up at Fraser. Before he could erupt, Adolphus broke in genially. "Oh, I wouldn't bother if I were you. Elizabeth is up to all rigs and fancies. She'll put a flea in your ear soon enough." He turned to Elizabeth with a great creaking of stays. "Wouldn't you, my dumpling?"

Elizabeth, thus adjured and not liking the term of endearment one bit, smiled sweetly. "Oh, I have a heart of flint. Nothing could turn my head short of brute force."

"That is a possibility," murmured the captain. Fortunately, Elizabeth was directly behind him at the heavily laden sideboard, and only she could hear the provocative statement.

"What was that you said, Captain?" Sumner demanded suspiciously.

"Whatever it was, it set her to blushing," Adolphus observed maddeningly. "It isn't often someone can make Elizabeth blush. You'll have to tell me how you do it, Captain. In private, of course."

Elizabeth resisted the temptation of taking the silver bowl of fluffy scrambled eggs and turning it upside down on someone's head for the simple reason that she couldn't decide who deserved it the most. Sumner with his handsome face like a thundercloud, Adolphus with his self-satisfied smirk in the midst of his great moon face, or the totally infuriating Captain Fraser.

Sumner and Adolphus obviously had tried to outdo themselves in piggery when they helped themselves to the breakfast buffet. Elizabeth, who by this time had digested the pre-prandial cinnamon buns and after her brisk walk was completely ravenous, was about to load her plate in a similar fashion when she espied Fraser's ascetic meal. A piece of dried toast, partially eaten, and a cup of black coffee seemed enough for the noble captain. Sighing, Elizabeth helped herself to a solitary piece of toast, poured herself a cup of coffee without her usual lashings of cream and sugar, and took her place at the table.

"Is that all you're going to eat?" demanded Sumner with the usual tact of brothers.

"I had something earlier," she said between her teeth. "This will be quite sufficient."

"It never was before, no matter what you'd eaten previously," Sumner replied, taking leave to doubt her. "You must be slimming again. I would have thought you'd wait till we got home to try and take off a bit of weight. You must have a maggot in your brain."

Elizabeth, goaded past endurance, kicked her brother sharply under the table. Unfortunately, she hit Captain Fraser instead, who jerked with a muttered curse and turned to stare at her out of amazed eyes.

"I beg your pardon," she said breathlessly, turning even rosier. "I thought that was my brother's leg."

"Tried to kick me, did you?" Sumner sniffed. "I've warned you about that, my girl. Serves you right that you got Captain Fraser instead."

"I hardly think so," Fraser said in his slow, deep voice.

"Well, you wouldn't," Sumner observed amiably. "I tell you, Fraser, you're lucky you don't have a sister. They're mean as snakes and the very devil to live with."

"As a matter of fact, I have three sisters," Michael said evenly. "All as charming as your lovely sister."

"You think her charming, eh?" Sumner demanded through grilled kidneys. "Try living with her."

Michael bowed. "I would be most honored, but I doubt the lady would be agreeable."

To Michael's obvious surprise, Elizabeth greeted this with an uncontrolled chuckle. Doing her best to keep a straight face, she glared at her unrepentant brother. "Before you go offering me about, Sumner, I would suggest you ask my opinion. Charming as Captain Fraser may be, I would still prefer to live with Miss Biddleford."

"Your old governess?" Adolphus blurted in tones of deepest horror. "Jeremy would never hear of it! Absolutely out of the question, my dear. Think what people would say; a young creature like yourself setting up housekeeping like a veritable antidote. You ain't at your last prayers yet. Three and twenty ain't such a great age, you know. Many ladies have married later and still had a full life."

Elizabeth didn't know whether to laugh or cry. Not that she should care that Adolphus and Sumner were painting her as a plump old maid to Michael Fraser. The opinion of a spy and a traitor, or at the very least a rude young man, could hardly matter to her. She gave Adolphus a steely look. "How sweet of you to say so, Adolphus," she said affably. "And I assure you, if you decided to fast for several months and wore tighter corsets, you might still be able to find yourself a bride at the advanced age of forty."

Adolphus's smile never left his face, though the pale blue eyes narrowed, and Sumner laughed through the grilled kidneys. "Warned you, didn't I, Dolph?" he chuckled. "Tongue on the girl like a viper. I pity the poor fool that makes her an offer. What do you think, Fraser?"

By this time Elizabeth was completely miserable, wondering if she had been too sharp with Adolphus and if her brother had deliberately set out to paint her in such an unflattering light. Staring numbly down at her dried-up toast, she felt a gentle kick on her ankle that could only have come from Fraser's Hessian-shod toe. She looked up, and he smiled at her, a completely dazzling smile that left her staring at him like a complete fool.

"I pity the man who wouldn't make her an offer," he said. And Elizabeth, throwing twenty-three years of caution to the wind, smiled back.

Chapter 8

"JUST WHERE DO you think you are going, young lady?"

Lady Elfreda's piercing tones echoed through the massive hallway, rattling the random suits of armor and causing the baronial pennants far overhead to waft in the breeze. "And in your riding habit? After a full luncheon, a lady usually requires at least an hour's rest on her bed. Brenna and that contessa creature are resting up for this evening's festivities. Or had you forgotten we're having a few couples in for dancing and cards?"

"I haven't forgotten, and I'm looking forward to it enormously," Elizabeth answered, lying blithely. "So much so, in fact, that I know I couldn't possibly sleep a wink if I were to lie down, so I thought I might go for a ride this afternoon. Just down to the sea and back."

"We don't have any suitable horses for a lady to ride," Lady Elfreda said sternly, her tone suggesting that the term "lady" was only a matter of courtesy.

Elizabeth slapped her riding crop against her heavy lavender skirts in mock dismay. "Oh, what a shame. I suppose I shall have to make do with a walk in the garden with Adolphus. It's turned into such a lovely day, and you know what they say: spring is the most romantic time of year."

"Of course, there's always the new mare Adolphus brought for Brenna," Lady Elfreda said immediately. "A trifle restive, perhaps. I don't know if you're enough of a horsewoman to manage her." The milky blue eyes gleamed beneath the crepe-like lids.

Elizabeth rose to the bait as swiftly as Lady Elfreda had. "I would think that if Brenna can manage, I certainly could."

Lady Elfreda permitted herself a small smile. "No doubt. Inform the groom that I told you to ride Lacey. I am certain you'll have an entertaining ride."

The groom, however, had his doubts, as did Elizabeth when she espied the high-strung, nervous creature that danced about in the cobbled stable-yard while the poor lad tried to saddle her.

"She's not the world's best-tempered beast, Miss Traherne," he said apologetically. "Are you sure you wouldn't rather have another one? We've any number of gentler mounts more suitable for a lady."

"Not according to Lady Elfreda," Elizabeth said wryly. "Never mind. If she thinks I'm up to riding Lacey, I certainly wouldn't want to prove her wrong. Ah . . . has anyone else gone out riding today?" She tried to keep her voice casually interested.

The boy scratched his tousled head. "Not as far as I know, miss. Not yet, at least. Will ye be wanting me to come with ye?"

"Not today, thank you. You needn't worry. I'm used to taking care of myself, and I don't intend to go far. Just down to the sea." She hesitated for a moment. "If you wouldn't mind, don't mention to anyone that I've gone out. I'm not in the mood for company, and I wouldn't want anyone to think they had to catch up with me."

"Very good, miss. Mum's the word."

Lacey proved to be as much of a handful as Elizabeth had expected. Fortunately, the three dashing Trahernes were as noted for their horsemanship as for their good looks. Once out in the open countryside, she gave Lacey her head, and they raced across the stubbled fields at a spanking pace, the wind whipping through her hair and sending it streaming along behind her. Once a hoyden, always a hoyden, she thought with no real regret, giving herself up to the sheer pleasure of the sunny day, the wind in her face, and the feel of a strong, beautiful animal beneath her.

Starfield Cove was a reasonable distance from Winfields, a distance that seemed far shorter on Lacey's back. Steep hills led down to the rocky shore, crisscrossed with rough pathways better suited to goats than human beings. A few scraggly pines provided a doubtful shelter, but the rock formations, which doubtless had shielded smugglers in the past and would do so again, would provide admirable cover for an inquisitive young lady. Tethering the exhausted and somewhat quieter Lacey at a good distance, she made her way down the sloping pathway, the pebbles rolling beneath her riding boots and several times threatening to send her plunging downward into the sea.

Stopping about halfway down, she found a comfortable spot behind a large outcropping of rock. It couldn't have been a better spot, with a perfect view of the shoreline. The only disadvantage was the distance to the sea for her myopic eyes, but then, she didn't care to be in the traitors' laps. The spot was both sunny and covered with soft, cushiony moss, and the headlong dash to the sea had tired her. Elizabeth, curling up against the rock to wait for her prey, fell sound asleep.

"WHAT IN GOD'S name are you doing here?"

The voice broke through her pleasant dreams, and her eyes flew open to view the object of those reveries, albeit looking a great deal more grim and unfriendly than he had a few moments ago when Elizabeth had been in the arms of Morpheus. She stared up at Michael Fraser out of sleepy eyes, uncomfortably aware of her unbound hair, the two buttons undone at the top of her prim lavender habit, and her unexplainable presence.

"I . . . I beg your pardon?" she stammered, stalling for time, looking about uneasily. Down at the shoreline, too far away for her to make out any features, stood a man. Taller than Wat Simpkin and strangely familiar was the mysterious Mr. Fredericks. He stared up at them with a wary intentness that communicated itself to Elizabeth's startled eyes.

"I said, what in God's name are you doing here?" Michael demanded roughly, reclaiming her attention.

A moment later she found herself yanked quite brutally to her feet. She stood there, squinting at him through the blazing sunlight as he deliberately stationed himself between her and the shoreline, his broad back obscuring her vision, and she felt a momentary rush of panic. He was suspected of killing at least one man, he was no doubt a desperate spy, and he looked frankly murderous at the moment. It would not take much: a rough shove that would send her hurtling down the pathway to the sea and the feet of his confederate, probably breaking her neck; a blow on the side of the head; those tanned, strong hands reaching around her throat. . . .

Those hands grabbed her arm in a fierce grip and began dragging her back up the hill at a rapid pace. Looking back toward the shoreline, she could see no trace of the man who had been staring up at them just moments ago.

"Do you have the faintest idea," Michael was demanding in a furious voice, "just how dangerous this game you're playing is? It's not an anagram or a French novel; it's a life or death proposition."

"What is?" she demanded weakly, struggling to keep up with him. "I just went for a peaceful ride down to the sea. What's the harm in that?"

"You know damned well what the harm in it is," he said roughly. "You expect me to believe you? That you just happened to choose Starfield Cove when there are a number of nearer, more congenial accesses to the sea you could have ridden to? You expect me to believe that you just happened to tether your horse out of sight and went to hide behind a boulder for want of something better to do?"

"I thought there might be some early wild strawberries," she said defensively.

Fraser stopped dead still, and Elizabeth, still moving at his breakneck pace, barreled into him full force. He caught her before she fell, holding her at arm's length. The grim expression had softened somewhat, and there was a reluctant quirk to his well-shaped mouth. "I could almost believe you, Elizabeth. For your sake I'd like to, but I don't dare. If you do not curb your meddling and obviously insatiable curiosity, I will have to lock you in your room."

She stared up at him in amazement. "I didn't give you leave to call me by my given name," she said lamely.

"No, you didn't. And as a matter of fact, I don't think I will. Elizabeth is far too formal for a ramshackle female such as you.

You're a Lizzie if ever I saw one."

"I'm Miss Traherne," she shot back, at a loss to deal with this abrupt change in personality.

"What you are is damnably interfering, and I can't afford to waste my time and energies looking out for you," he said frankly. They were at the top of the cliff by this time, and Lacey eyed her with deceptive passivity from her spot beside Fraser's huge black stallion.

"You aren't going to get away with it, you know," Elizabeth said abruptly, daringly. "Someone will catch you before you can find the papers. Sir Henry, or the general, or someone will stop you."

The expression on his tanned face was more harassed than dangerous. "Aided and abetted by you, no doubt," he said wearily. "Leave it alone, Lizzie. If you don't, I can't answer for the consequences."

"Is that a threat?" she asked in steady tones, trying to ignore the pleasure she felt in the sound of his deep, slow voice saying "Lizzie."

"More in the nature of a warning. I'm not about to satisfy your immense curiosity by giving you any explanations or excuses. You've somehow managed to stumble onto far too much knowledge already, and the less you know, the better. Be a good girl and mind your own business, and everything might possibly come 'round right in the end."

The look Elizabeth cast at him out of mutinous brown eyes was far from reassuring. With an irritated explosion of breath he put his hands on her slender waist and threw her onto Lacey's broad back. Elizabeth scarcely had time to catch hold of the saddle when the nervy beast reared up with a shrill whinny and took off, yanking the tethered reins free from the scraggly branch where she had tied them.

This ride was a great deal different from the one on the way to the ocean. If Lacey had run fast the last time, she flew now, with the reins trailing and completely out of Elizabeth's reach. Too fast for her to try jumping off onto the spongy turf, she thought with a very real panic. Michael Fraser might very well be responsible for her death, after all.

Her hands were slippery with sweat as she clung to the saddle, and she remembered with despair her riding gloves, resting no doubt beneath that boulder. Her legs were numb, and each jolt and bump threatened to toss her headfirst from the animal's terrified back. Numbly Elizabeth realized that she couldn't hold on much longer.

Through blinded eyes she was vaguely aware of a figure coming up on her right. Michael, his stallion thundering beneath him, drew even with her maddened beast. Leaning over at a dangerous angle, he made a grab for the trailing reins and missed. The stallion fell back a few paces, and Lacey, even more terrified, sped up, bugling a high, panicked shriek.

Once again he drew even, halfway swinging out of his saddle as he reached for the reins. This time he caught them, and slowly, imperceptibly Elizabeth felt the horse slow in response to the steady, inexorable pressure on the reins. Finally Lacey came to a shuddering halt, her flanks heaving, her eyes rolling, winded, exhausted, unrepentant.

Elizabeth slid from her back. Michael was there to catch her as her legs buckled. Burying her face against his shoulder, she put her arms around his neck and held on, her breath coming in frightened sobs as she trembled in his tight clasp.

After a long, long time the panic left her, her breathing was regular, and if her heart still pounded too rapidly, well, she had never been held in a man's arms before. Regretfully she loosened her hold, and immediately he set her free. Pushing her hair away from her damp, flushed face, she looked up at him and managed a shaky smile. "Thank you," she said, and found it coming out in a hoarse croak.

"Thank you?" he echoed bitterly. "Of all the stupid things to have done! Do you realize that you could have been killed?"

Her temper flared. "It was hardly my fault. You were the one who threw me on the horse. I couldn't help it if you frightened her."

"I realize that," he said stiffly. "I wouldn't have thought you would have been out riding a horse that was scarcely broken in."

"Lady Elfreda's suggestion," Elizabeth said with a wry grin. "I should have known better than to have listened to that . . . that gorgon."

She was rewarded with a reluctant smile. "I could have killed you," he said, self-recrimination still strong in his voice, and the dark eyes were troubled.

So much for him being a conscienceless killer, Elizabeth thought triumphantly. There had been an imperceptible change in their relationship in the last few moments, one she couldn't understand but welcomed anyway. She smiled up impishly at him. "You still could."

She was met with an answering gleam in his eyes. "And no doubt you'll continue to drive me in that direction. Still and all, I think I'd be more likely to do it with my bare hands the next time I catch you where you don't belong."

"I'll take that under advisement," she said demurely, "and make sure that you don't catch me."

"Lizzie—"

"Will you help me back on this crazed beast?" she interrupted swiftly.

He stared at her, saying nothing for a long moment. "You're intending to ride her back to Winfields?" he demanded finally.

"Well, I'm not intending to walk," she said with some asperity. "If you're just a touch gentler, I should have no difficulty. She may not be cowed, but I expect she's too tired to run off again." As if in agreement, Lacey nodded, her eyes rolling more lazily.

There was an arrested expression on Fraser's face as he stared down at her.

"I suppose you think I'm completely unladylike," she said resignedly. "But what good would it do if I were to have the vapors all over the place? I have to get back to Winfields some way or another, and I'd as soon not sit around in the grass while you return with a carriage or some such fustian."

"You misunderstand me. I seldom encounter more sense than sensibility in a young lady."

This wasn't quite as endearing as Elizabeth could have hoped. "Oh, yes, I have a great deal of sense," she responded cheerfully. "It is extremely difficult to overset me."

"Is it?" he wondered aloud, his eyes playing on her face in a curiously disturbing manner. "At some other place and time I might endeavor to prove you wrong."

"You would have a difficult time doing so," she said firmly, deliberately daring him. "You forget I am past my first youth."

"A veritable woman of the world, in fact," he said softly, that bewitching smile playing about his lips. "We shall see, Lizzie."

"And I suggest you refrain from calling me that," she said sternly. "Sumner wouldn't like it in the slightest."

"Yes, ma'am," he replied, agreeing meekly. "Are you ready to go back now?"

"More than ready."

Once more his strong hands went around her waist. Very slowly he lifted her until her face was level with his. He held her there for a long moment, her feet dangling in midair. Her breath was coming rapidly, and Michael's eyes were alight with amusement.

"Are you certain I should have such difficulty ruffling that mature calm of yours?" he questioned softly, and his breath was warm and sweet on her flushed face.

"Very certain," she responded, lying firmly. For a long moment he held her there. He's going to kiss me, she thought, and then I *shall* faint.

A moment later she was in the saddle once more, unkissed. Lacey edged about with a trace of her previous nervousness, but the headlong flight had taken its toll on her energy, and she stood there peaceably enough after the initial start. Elizabeth controlled her absurd feeling of disappointment nobly. "Would you care to race back?" she inquired with deceptive calm.

"No, thank you. You may be a nerveless creature, but I am not so sturdy. One wild race across these fields is more than enough for one afternoon." He took one of her hands in his strong hand and held it for a moment. "Where are your gloves?"

"Back by the boulder."

"You'll have blisters by the time we get back to Winfields," he warned.

"If that's the worst I suffer from today's adventures, I shall consider myself lucky."

His eyes were very blue in the bright afternoon sunlight that beat down on her back through the lavender habit that now had a long rent under one arm. "Will you promise me one thing?" he asked softly. "That you will behave yourself for the next two days?"

"Would you believe me if I did?" she countered.

"If you promised."

"Then it is a great shame I cannot promise what I have no intention of doing," she said sweetly, and gave Lacey a gentle nudge toward home.

Chapter 9

HAD IT NOT BEEN for Brenna O'Shea, Elizabeth would have managed to sneak up to her room with no one the wiser of her afternoon's strenuous activities. She was on the first step in the hallway off Lady Elfreda's study when Brenna appeared, taking in her disheveled appearance with wide eyes and a mouth shaped like an O.

"What in the world happened to you?" she asked.

Elizabeth was acutely aware of her tumbled hair, the large rent in the seam of her jacket, her flushed face, and the twigs clinging to her crumpled skirt. "I'll tell you later. I want to get up and change before anyone else sees me. Where is everyone?"

"Adolphus and Sir Maurice are in the library with Sir Henry Hatchett and his assistant, really the most handsome young man. They arrived a short while ago. Apparently Lady Beatrice is indisposed. Lady Elfreda's in her study, sound asleep, thank heavens. Sumner and the contessa have gone for a walk, and I have no idea where Captain Fraser might be." The green eyes made it clear that she could make a very good guess.

"Sumner and the contessa have gone for a walk?" Elizabeth echoed, picking up on the most important part. "Why in the world would he do any such thing?"

"He appears to admire her greatly," Brenna said with an airy unconcern that fooled Elizabeth for not one moment.

"He must have windmills in his head," she said frankly. "I'll have a talk with him when he comes in."

"I beg you, don't! If he doesn't wish to be with me, then I must abide by his decision. Perhaps I refined too much on small attentions he paid me in the past. I can scarcely compete with someone as beautiful or glamorous as the contessa."

"Who are you talking to?" Lady Elfreda's irritable voice bellowed from a nearby room, followed by the owner. The tall, angular figure towered over the two girls, and Elizabeth noticed with amusement that her coiffure had slipped a bit, revealing, as she had always suspected, that her ladyship wore a wig.

For a moment she had forgotten her own appearance. The satisfied expression on Lady Elfreda's seamed face reminded her swiftly. "Took a toss, did you?" she inquired affably. "I knew you would. Serves you right." She turned to Brenna, pinching her arm sharply to ensure herself of the girl's attention. "This chit insisted she was capable of riding Lacey. I warned her she would be too much to handle, but would she listen? Not Miss Elizabeth Traherne! Who would have thought a vicar's sister would be such an irresponsible hoyden? I do hope Adolphus didn't see you in such a dreadful state. He can't abide untidiness." She peered hopefully over her shoulder for a sight of her portly son.

Elizabeth had a brief struggle with her temper and, for the moment, won. "Don't bother your head about it, Lady Elfreda. I am perfectly all right, and Adolphus is with the gentlemen in the library, Brenna informs me. He has no idea that I had a small accident."

"You should never have insisted on riding Lacey," Brenna said with great seriousness. "Both Lady Elfreda and I could have told you she's far too wild for anyone to ride yet. You could have been killed."

Elizabeth looked at Lady Elfreda's cold face and detected not the slightest trace of remorse. "You're absolutely right, Brenna," she said calmly. "It was unwise in the extreme of me not to pay more attention to Lady Elfreda's dubious advice. I will be a great deal more careful the next time."

"Elizabeth!" Sumner's shocked tones carried to her ears, and she controlled a start of irritation. A moment later her elegantly clad brother had joined the group of women, with the contessa holding back, watching them all with a trace of amusement. "What in heaven's name has happened to you?" he demanded, his normally mellifluous voice high-pitched in outrage. "Don't you know better than to go around looking like some sort of . . . of . . ." Words failed him, as they usually did. Elizabeth noted absently the golden hair and angry blue eyes, the beautifully shaped nostrils flaring as they always did when he was angry with her. Not for the first time she wondered why a cruel fate would give her boring brother the prettiest face in the family.

"I was trying to get to my room," she said calmly. "And if everyone would stop asking me what happened, I would do so."

"But what did happen?" cried her brother with singular obtuseness, and Elizabeth wondered how a sensible, pretty girl such as Brenna could possibly love such a creature, no matter how angelically fair.

She smiled up at him limpidly. "Lady Elfreda sent me out on a dangerous horse, and I fell."

"Elizabeth!" Sumner gasped in horrified accents. "I am shocked and saddened to hear you speak in such a way of this good kind lady who is our hostess. Your want of sensibility has often distressed me, but never so much as now. I am grieved by your levity and only hope dear, kind Lady Elfreda will forgive you."

Dear, kind Lady Elfreda smirked. "Do not distress yourself, Sumner. Your sister is a trifle overset by her accident. No doubt when she has time to rest and reflect, she will regret her lack of manners and apologize."

"Elizabeth!" Sumner said sternly. "I want you to apologize to Lady Elfreda *immediately*. You will not go up to your room until you have begged this kind woman's pardon."

"Sumner," she replied in deceptively dulcet tones, "you and Lady Elfreda may go to the devil." And turning her back on them, she moved upstairs with an understandable alacrity, leaving her brother sputtering and fuming behind her.

DINNER WAS A TRIFLE delayed that evening as a result of the belated appearance of their host. While Lady Elfreda tapped one overlarge foot on the Aubusson-carpeted marble floor and Sumner flirted almost desperately with a willing contessa,

Elizabeth found a comfortable spot somewhat out of the way of the action and observed those around her.

She was dressed in one of her new silk gowns, the one with the greatest amount of décolletage showing off her admirable breasts and shoulders. The dull gold of the silk made her brown eyes appear almost sherry-colored, and her slightly tawny skin glowed in the candlelight. She was pardonably secure in the knowledge that she was in her best looks, her afternoon adventure having produced no deleterious effect other than a few blisters on her palms from riding without gloves. She folded the offending hands peacefully in her lap.

She was just as glad, she told herself, that Michael was off in the corner talking with Brenna. Not a glance in her direction had he bestowed. No looks of glazed admiration, not even that small, mocking smile that held a world of meaning acknowledged the elegance of her toilette. And now he stood towering over the tiny Irish girl, his eyes rapt, his attention totally absorbed.

The same could hardly be said of Brenna. Whenever she could, she would cast a surreptitious glance at Sumner's bemused face, and the misery in her fine green eyes would have been apparent to a complete moonling, Elizabeth thought angrily. *Doesn't Fraser realize she wants to be left alone? And doesn't he realize that I would like to give him a piece of my mind?*

Sir Henry Hatchett hadn't been much of a reassurance either. He had proved to be a short, round little man, with a cheerful expression about his myopic eyes, a drooping white mustache and side whiskers, and a slight Scots accent. His wife, Lady Beatrice, he had explained with a faint burr, had become indisposed and would be unable to join them. Elizabeth had thought it somewhat odd that Sir Henry had come on ahead with his adjutant, but no odder than his preoccupied, absentminded behavior. He seemed hardly the type to hold a high position in the Foreign Office, as Sumner had whispered to her importantly, and Elizabeth wondered if, as usual, her brother had merely been claiming more intimate knowledge of a situation than he actually possessed.

All in all, Sir Henry Hatchett inspired no confidence in Elizabeth's worried breast. She could no more unburden the tangle of information that had come her inquisitive way this long day than she could have confided in the forbidding General Wingert. At least, not yet. She would give Michael a little more time to inspire her with confidence. As her eyes swept over the planes and shadows of his tanned face, she uttered a tiny sigh.

The one real improvement in the status quo of the houseparty moved to her side, and she smiled up at him welcomingly, hoping that the wretched Captain Fraser would notice.

Sir Henry Hatchett's right-hand man was none other than Rupert St. Ives, Jeremy's roommate at Oxford and one of Elizabeth and Sumner's oldest friends. When Elizabeth first entered the drawing room, conscious of her elegance and determined to be cool and remote, she'd taken one look at Rupert's tall, familiar figure and let out an unladylike shriek of joy.

"Rupert!" Ignoring Fraser's quizzical expression, she had run across the room and flung herself on Rupert's broad chest, into arms that were only too happy to welcome her. Even Sumner had left off his elaborate posturings to greet Captain St. Ives with real pleasure, pumping his hand and begging his sister to "leave off crushing the poor fellow."

"Why such a sigh, Elizabeth?" he questioned now in an undertone. "And such a pensive look?"

"I was thinking about Jeremy," she said mendaciously, and then felt swamped with guilt as Rupert's handsome face looked suitably grave. She *should* be thinking more about Jeremy and about what villains such as Michael Fraser could do to his safety if they weren't stopped in time.

"You haven't heard from him in a while, then?" he questioned.

"Not a word for weeks."

"Well, from my experience let me tell you that usually means that all is well. With any luck old Jem will be back with us by summer."

"Oh, do you really think so?" she questioned eagerly. "I

confess we've both been terribly worried these last months."

"Yes, I really think so," he said firmly, and Elizabeth smiled up at him gratefully, noticing for not the first time in her life how very attractive he was.

Rupert St. Ives was a military man from the tips of his well-shod feet to the top of his well-cropped brown hair. He was just a bit over medium height, but his soldier's bearing lent the impression of added height, and the broad shoulders, trim waist, and well-turned legs appeared to advantage in uniform. His hazel eyes had an uncomfortably sharp expression in them when they dwelled on most people, his mouth was a thin, determined line, and the jaw was just a trifle too decisive, especially coupled with a hawk-like nose. But on the rare occasions when he smiled, he could appear quite charming, and Elizabeth, having known him since childhood and having survived a desperate crush on him at the tender age of fifteen, still had a latent tendency to think him a veritable Adonis. Although Mars might be more apt, she thought now, looking at him with more impartial eyes.

"Tell me, Elizabeth, how long has that fellow been here?" he requested suddenly in a disapproving voice.

"Whoever do you mean?" she questioned with a great show of innocence, knowing perfectly well the object of his censure.

"Michael Fraser. I can't imagine what he's doing here. The man's got a terrible reputation. I hate to see you having to be polite to him. I, for one, have no intention of having anything to do with him."

"What's so terrible about him?" she queried.

"Now is hardly the time to tell you. But I don't trust him, and I'm amazed that an astute old soldier like Maurice Wingert tolerates him on his staff." He shook his closely cropped head reprovingly.

"But what . . ."

A sudden lull in the quiet hum of conversation told them that their host had arrived. Looking up toward the door, Elizabeth was for once in her life struck dumb.

Sir Adolphus Wingert had outdone himself that evening. Attired in ells and ells of pale pink satin trimmed with falls of the finest Mechlin lace, he made an astounding figure. Despite the tight lacing that announced itself with a great creaking at his every move, his formidable stomach, adorned with a waistcoat of ivory embroidered with tiny blue forget-me-nots and golden fleurs-de-lis, and the generous jowls that drooped gracefully over the high shirt points and rested carefully on the intricate folds of a tie that Elizabeth recognized with her usual acumen as Dolph's rendition of the Oriental, proclaimed him as a man of great appetite.

His pale pink unmentionables clung to voluptuous thighs, the clocks on his silk stockings matched his waistcoat, and a lace garter adorned with rosettes decorated one plump calf.

The pale moon face was carefully shaved, the thinning blond hair was thickly pomaded and swept into an arrangement that Elizabeth failed to put a name to, and from one pendulous earlobe dangled a large diamond earring.

As he paused to allow his assembled guests to fully appreciate his sartorial magnificence, he flicked open his snuffbox, cunningly designed to resemble a small casket, and applied his favorite mixture of snuff to one nostril with the expedient of a tiny silver shovel. Sneezing delicately, he blinked his pale, watering eyes and smiled benevolently on his assembled guests.

The assembled guests were speechless. Clearly, Adolphus expected praise and admiration for his turnout; clearly, no one felt able to voice such approval. As the silence lengthened and Adolphus's moon face lost some of its benevolent glow and began to turn sulky, Elizabeth gave herself a small shake.

Rising from her seat, she gave Adolphus the dazzling smile that had won more than one man's heart and had the ability to bring forth a furious frown from the watching Michael Fraser.

"You needn't expect, dear Dolph," she said lightly, "that any of the ladies will have a thing to do with you. It is wicked and unconscionable and a great deal too bad of you to outshine us so. We all look like drab hags compared to you. Unfair and uncivil of you, Dolph." She leaned up and kissed him in a cousinly fashion on one plump cheek, which promptly turned pink to match his ensemble.

"Yes, indeed," Sumner added smoothly, belatedly realizing which side his bread was buttered on. "You look absolutely glorious. I doubt the Prince Regent has anything quite so fine. You quite outshine us all, yes indeed."

Adolphus bestowed a gracious smile upon his vicar. "You're quite correct, Sumner. Prinny's clothes are positively shabby compared to this. Thought I'd do the ladies honor by wearing it."

The ladies did their best to look honored, while Lady Elfreda rose to her full height. "Well," she said in frosty tones. "I suppose we may finally eat, Adolphus?"

"But of course, Mama," he said indulgently, reassured as to his loveliness. "Contessa?" He held out one plump arm, and that lady accepted it, smiling demurely into his rosy face.

The couples arranged themselves swiftly. Too swiftly, Elizabeth thought disgruntledly. Lady Elfreda immediately commandeered both elderly gentlemen, Brenna grabbed for an absentminded Sumner, and Elizabeth, by rising and greeting Adolphus, found herself squarely in between the two remaining gentlemen, Michael Fraser and Rupert St. Ives. They both moved swiftly, but Fraser was the faster of the two. She found that she had no choice but to accept his arm, despite the belligerent glower on his tanned face. But apparently the glower was for Rupert, not her.

"You know, you needn't accept Fraser as your dinner partner, Elizabeth," he said coldly, ignoring Michael completely.

"Miss Traherne knows that perfectly well," Michael replied, placing a possessive hand over hers as it rested on his arm. She had little doubt that if she tried to pull away, the fingers would tighten unmercifully.

"If you'd prefer not to associate with traitors, Elizabeth, you could take my arm," Rupert grated out.

The fingers tightened anyway as rage flooded Fraser's usually impassive face. "Are you interested in fighting for the lady, St. Ives?"

"I have some consideration for my hostess," he replied stiffly. "I am waiting to hear from Elizabeth."

Elizabeth found that despite the nervousness such a bellicose air was arousing in the area of her stomach, she was actually enjoying having two exceedingly handsome gentlemen fight over her. But she knew she would be deceiving herself if she really believed Elizabeth Traherne was the bone of contention between these two snarling beasts.

"Captain Fraser claimed me first, Rupert," she said gently. "If my hostess accepts him, then I must do so too."

"Very well, Elizabeth. But remember, I'll be nearby if you require assistance." He marched out of the room without a backward glance, leaving Elizabeth alone with Michael Fraser. There was a dangerous expression on his face, one that didn't soften when he looked down at his dinner partner. He wasn't wearing his uniform tonight, and his somber black coat did nothing to detract from the strong back and shoulders. Here was one who'd have no need of corsets and buckram padding in his shoulders. The only thing that would improve him, Elizabeth thought objectively, would be a more amiable nature. He glowered down at her as disagreeably as he had glowered at Rupert, and she responded with an impish smile.

"Are we going to be at dagger drawing again?" she inquired. "I thought we had declared some sort of truce this afternoon."

"Then you mistook the matter. What happened this afternoon was an even stronger declaration of war. Unless you've thought better of my suggestion and decided to keep that delightful nose out of things that don't concern you."

Elizabeth couldn't resist reaching to touch that feature, having never had the felicity of hearing it described as delightful in her short life. "I hadn't realized it was merely a suggestion on your part," she said sweetly. "It sounded more like an order to me."

"An order you chose to ignore."

"I don't happen to be your subaltern, Captain," she fired back. "I'm certain there's nothing you'd like better than to have me under you and forced to obey your commands." The moment the unfortunate words were out of her mouth, she stopped, horrified, a deep red suffusing her features.

Fraser smiled down at her, a glint of laughter in his eyes. "I am certain you would rather have me not reply to that remark," he said gently, his low, deep voice amused.

"Yes," she said in a strangled tone of voice. They had almost reached the great dining hall. Surely he wouldn't say anything outrageous as long as they were in earshot of the others.

"Let me know when you'd like an answer to that question, Lizzie," he requested calmly. "Perhaps once this weekend is over."

She could feel the betraying color subsiding as he held the chair for her. "Yes," she said limpidly. "I shall be very busy this weekend." She smiled up at him defiantly.

Chapter 10

IT WAS A SPUR of the moment thing, Elizabeth realized, and foolish beyond permission. Lady Elfreda had ordered her guests into the ballroom. General Wingert had started off alone, and Elizabeth, hoping to gain some insight into the enigma of Michael Fraser, followed the elderly gentleman willy-nilly into a long deserted hallway running along the side of the gardens.

"General Wingert, I wonder if you could help me?" she began in her prettiest tone of voice, running to catch up with him.

The stout little fellow turned and stared reassuringly at Elizabeth out of dark, protuberant eyes as he ran his tongue over his thin pink lips. "And which chit are you, hey?" he barked, moving closer and pressing that large, commanding stomach against her. "Not a favorite of m'sister's, are you, gel?"

As she tried to edge away, one pudgy, surprisingly strong hand reached out and caught her arm in a viselike grip, and he moved even closer. He exuded an unpleasant odor of a nauseatingly sweet cologne, his fingers dug into the tender flesh of her arm, and to her amazement and indignation she felt a fumbling hand reach behind and pinch her.

"Why don't we take a small stroll in the garden? We can talk out there. I'll help you, and then you can help me," the general suggested in a tone that failed to allow for refusal. "Nice night, and you're a taking thing. A bit too tall, but you've a demmed nice figger." And he began pulling her toward the French doors off the hallway as Elizabeth foundered helplessly for excuses.

"General Wingert!" Like a *deus ex achine*, Michael Fraser's voice broke through the aging lecher's concentration, and with a particularly foul curse he released Elizabeth so abruptly that she fell back against the wall, staring in wonder as Fraser caught up with his superior. "Sir Henry wondered if you could spare him a few moments, sir. He says it's urgent."

The general's beady little eyes ran over Elizabeth's trembling figure with a lingering glance. "Not now, Fraser," he barked. "Can't you see I'm busy?"

The rebuke didn't faze Michael in the slightest. "Yes, sir. But Sir Henry was quite insistent."

"What was he insistent about?" The contessa's lazily amused voice drifted past them as her elegant, black-clad figure moved into the hallway. "There you are, Miss Traherne! I had been wondering where you got to. Your brother tells me you play divinely, and unfortunately Lady Elfreda failed to arrange for musicians. We cannot dance unless we can prevail upon your generosity." Taking the same arm that the general had so recently manhandled, she led Elizabeth down the corridor without a backward glance.

Once they were out of earshot, she dropped Elizabeth's arm, the feline smile still in place. "You ought to watch out for the general, my dear. He has a fancy for very young ladies. I wouldn't suggest you encourage him. He has some rather exotic habits that I fear would both alarm and disgust you. Much better to leave him to an old campaigner like me."

"Contessa, I assure you, I have no interest in the general whatsoever," Elizabeth stammered, both horrified and fascinated by the contessa's hints.

By that time Fraser had caught up with them, a fierce glower on his dark face. "If you don't watch your step, Miss Traherne, you'll have no say in the matter. The general isn't one to be balked of what he wants. Keep away from him."

Elizabeth's temper flared. "Is that an order?" she inquired sweetly.

"If you choose to see it that way," he rejoined. "Or you can see it merely as a piece of friendly advice."

"I hadn't realized you were my friend," she shot back, then bit her tongue as she caught the contessa's entertained expression. "I beg your pardon," she murmured, color high in her face. "I thank you both for your concern. I . . . I believe I'm needed in the ballroom." And she vanished into the room.

The contessa smiled up at Fraser, greatly amused. "So the wind sits in that direction, does it, my friend? How very interesting."

WHAT LADY ELFREDA had no doubt considered an absolute whirl of dissipated pleasures struck Elizabeth as deadly boring. Three couples had been added to the uncomfortable little party in order to make up several tables of whist and allow for dancing. As the three couples—the Marshbanks; Sir Junius Harford and his meek wife, Lady Helena; and the Dantons—were all of Lady Elfreda's generation and temperament, the additions were not a success. It was soon discovered that Elizabeth was the only guest who had the slightest claim to musicality, and therefore she found herself spending the next few hours after dinner playing the pianoforte with stolid determination while Sumner and Rupert took turns waltzing with the flirtatious contessa, Brenna suffered Adolphus to tread all over her toes, and the elderly couples played whist with gimlet-eyed determination. Michael looked on from a spot in the corner, not even offering, Elizabeth thought disconsolately, to turn the pages for her. She could comfort herself with the realization that at least he didn't choose to dance with the contessa.

One look at Brenna's great green eyes and the expression of acute misery therein convinced Elizabeth that her brother was even a greater fool than she had first imagined. If such a thing was possible, she added, missing a note in her amusement. If there was ever such a cod's head!

Another missed note, and Elizabeth redirected her attention to the pianoforte for a few moments. When she looked up again, Michael Fraser's tall, lean figure had disappeared from the wall where he had been leaning nonchalantly; he was nowhere in sight.

Immediately deciding that the man was up to no good, Elizabeth speeded up the tempo, disconcerting the couples no end, and then brought the waltz to an abrupt halt. She rose from the bench hastily before her audience could demand an encore that would give them an excuse to hold a member of the opposite sex in their arms for a longer period of time.

"I need a short rest," she said somewhat breathlessly as Sumner cast her a glowering look, reluctantly releasing the contessa's clinging black form. "Perhaps a breath of fresh air."

None of the gentlemen seemed disposed to accompany her, which, though offensive, was just as well. Adolphus had taken advantage of Sumner's temporary inattention and claimed the contessa's hand, and Sumner had more pressing duties than squiring his unencouraging sister about a spring-like garden. Besides, it was dashed raw out there. Even Rupert had wandered off to oversee the aging card players.

The terrace was deserted as Elizabeth made her solitary way across it. In the sparse moonlight the towers loomed in the distance above her head, giving her an uneasy little shiver of apprehension.

One of Winfields's most innovative and pretentious remodelers, the fourth Adolphus Wingert (the current incumbent was the sixth of that name), had decided that the Wingert family residence needed something truly impressive to inform the entire countryside of their consequence. Therefore, he had ordered the erection of four enormous towers of ancient Norman design at each corner of the rambling building. As it was the mid-eighteenth century, and Norman towers looked attractive only when they were crumbling, Adolphus had incorporated a cunningly crumbling effect over the stonework. Sadly enough, the crumbling had proved more thorough than one could have hoped so that, less than a hundred years later, all but one of them had been declared unsafe.

What better place, thought Elizabeth, to hide a packet of treasonous papers? No one would think to venture onto those massive battlements, and any manner of nefarious activities could be carried on without witness. The problem was, which of the four towers? The only sturdy one? Surely a desperate spy wouldn't allow a little moldering masonry to deter him. Throwing her shoulders back, Elizabeth strode onward into the garden, wishing belatedly that she had brought a shawl to cover her nearly nude chest and shoulders. The dull gold satin shone in the moonlight, but it was not fashioned for warmth, and the bright spring afternoon had given way to a rather chilly evening. Had she realized she would have a chance to pursue the mysterious doings, she would have dressed more carefully.

But the sight of Rupert had reminded her quite forcibly of Jeremy and her duty, and her flagging determination strengthened. The absurd décolletage had done her no good whatsoever, she thought grumpily, her slippers noiseless on the flagstone pathway, moving farther away from the noise and light of the drawing room. She shouldn't have allowed herself to put personal vanity and the shameful wish to appear attractive to the mysterious Captain Fraser ahead of her doubts. If only. . . .

"Were you by any chance looking for me?" A slow, deep voice came to her ear, and she stopped with a jerk, a small, nervous yelp coming from her throat before she could stop it.

"Really, Captain Fraser," she said severely when she had regained a semblance of control, "how you do frighten one! I had no idea you would be out on such a chilly night."

"You look a great deal chillier," he observed, with a pointed look at the expanse of moon-silvered flesh above the meager confines of her gown. "That's a very fetching gown, Lizzie, but I would watch out for Adolphus. He's the type to take a dress like that for a blatant invitation. He might be even worse than your friend the general."

It was fortunate that the moon was not quite full, for Elizabeth could feel her face suffuse with color. It had been an invitation, but definitely not for the portly, officious Adolphus.

"I'm afraid I don't find Adolphus as alarming as you obviously do, Captain," she said sweetly. "Without question he's slightly pompous."

"What you mean to say, despite this unusual roundaboutation on your part," Michael said sharply, "is that Dolph has more hair than wit and is nothing to worry about. But I think you underestimate him. I think Sir Adolphus Wingert could be quite formidable when crossed."

"I tremble in my boots," said Elizabeth pertly. "And what are you doing out here all alone? Up to no good, I don't doubt."

A small smile lit his dark face. "As a matter of fact, I slipped out to have a romantic assignation with a certain, lady of my acquaintance."

"Oh." She looked back toward the house, thoroughly embarrassed. "I didn't see anyone else leave."

The cynical smile deepened. "You must have scared her away."

There was no doubt he was laughing at her, an occurrence that Elizabeth found both irritating and beguiling. "Should I try to find her for you?" she questioned impishly, and then her warm brown eyes widened in shock. The expression on his face was something she had never seen before on a gentleman's face, and it boded no good for her.

"Don't bother," he said simply, with great determination. "You will provide an admirable substitute." And before she could collect her scattered wits, she found herself in his arms, being ruthlessly kissed.

Elizabeth had never been kissed before, although she had read countless descriptions of the experience in French novels that constituted the major portion of her reading material; but she was finding out rapidly that there was a great deal of difference between theory and actual experience. For one thing, actuality was far more delightful. His warm breath mingling with hers, the feel of his buttons pressing against her flesh, and the strength in those imprisoning arms were causing all sorts of astounding reactions in the pit of her stomach. He had had to force her chin up to kiss her, and it seemed only natural for her to reach up and put her arms around his neck while continuing this delightful pastime. It was with real regret that she felt him pull away somewhat, the strong arms still firmly around her waist as he looked down into her eyes. His eyes were filled with a curious expression; one might almost have called it tenderness. But then, the moonlight could be deceiving.

"Well, Lizzie," he said, and his voice was husky, "who would have thought?" And his mouth descended again.

If the first kiss had been a delightful surprise, this was something more of a shock. With a deftness of purpose that left her completely breathless he tilted her head back, slanting his mouth across hers, and the sudden, unmistakably raw passion both terrified and enchanted her. One of his strong, dark hands had left her waist to slide up the silky front of her dress, and as it caught the gentle swell of her breast, she stiffened in his arms, a small sound of reluctant protest issuing from the back of her throat.

He ignored it. His mouth was teasing, exciting hers, his tongue a sudden, shocking intruder into the warm haven of her mouth, and she felt her low-cut neckline slip lower still so that the cool night air chilled her flesh. Then his warm, rough-textured hands were touching her, holding her. She moaned into his mouth, a soft sound of both protest and desire, and his hands gentled on her sensitive flesh as his mouth finally released her.

"We're in real trouble, you know," he whispered. "I have to be out of my mind. This is neither the place nor the time, and you're most definitely not the woman."

She opened her mouth to protest, then shut it as sounds penetrated her love-dazed abstraction. With great snorting, heavy breathing, and noisy outrage, her host appeared on the scene. Sir Adolphus's pale, protruding blue eyes protruded even more, his thick, wet lips trembled with indignation, and his large front swelled with further outrage. "Cousin Elizabeth!" he thundered in awesome tones.

Michael's hands left her, pausing long enough to pull the dress back around her, and his tanned face was impassive as he faced Sir Adolphus's fire-breathing, chubby little form.

"I was warned, Fraser," continued Adolphus in high-pitched tones, "that you were unreliable, but I hardly thought I would have to put a guard on the female guests in my home! This poor frail creature that you've shabbily abused—"

"Gammon!" said Elizabeth roundly. "I haven't been shabbily abused. I—"

"Say no more, dear cousin Elizabeth!" he begged. "You are overcome by your experience, and who can blame you? I only thank heaven that Mama sent me out after you, else who knows what might have happened with a fellow so lost to every principle as to attack a poor flower of the female sex! I should have you horsewhipped, Fraser!"

"Would you stop this idiotic behavior?" begged Elizabeth, since Fraser made no move to defend himself. "Captain Fraser didn't attack me, Dolph. It just . . . happened. It was no one's fault, and there's no need to fall into a distemper'd freak about it."

Adolphus drew himself up to his full height, a mere inch shorter than Elizabeth's queenly form, and quivered with outrage. "Elizabeth, it grieves me to hear you defend this man. What your brother will say when I recount this night's deeds I shudder to think. I would say the best thing is for you to return to the house immediately. As for you, Fraser, I only wish there was something I could do to put you in your place. Obviously my hands are tied until this weekend is over, but don't think your superiors won't hear of this night's work!"

"I'm sure they'd be fascinated," he drawled.

Adolphus harrumphed. "All I can say is that Miss Traherne is obviously unwell, and I shall do all I can to persuade her to retire early and remove herself from your pernicious influence."

"Adolphus, you are being extremely tiresome," Elizabeth snapped. "Give me your arm, and we'll go back to the house. You are making a great fuss over nothing."

"Nothing?" echoed Fraser sotto voce, a gleam of laughter in his eyes. Fortunately, Adolphus was too overwrought to hear the teasing words.

With one glance of dislike the baron turned his broad back on the captain, catching Elizabeth's hand in a crushing grip and dragging her back toward the house, all the time uttering dire predictions under his breath. When Elizabeth looked back, Fraser was still standing there, watching them disappear. She could have wept with frustration. Now he could root about the towers as much as he wanted, with no fear that she would catch him in the act. If only she'd shown a little more resolution instead of allowing him to kiss her in that odious way!

Well, it wasn't precisely odious, she had to admit, as Adolphus's tight corsets and labored breathing forced him to advance at a slower pace, all the time haranguing her about her indecent behavior. As a matter of fact, it had been quite overwhelming. Her mouth and whole body still seemed to burn from his embrace. As she stumbled back onto the terrace behind Adolphus, she wondered whether she ought to experience that particular sensation again to see whether it would always be quite so enthralling. Merely on the basis of comparison, of course.

The first thing she had to do, however, was send Rupert out after Fraser. She hated to confide in St. Ives, though why she was so loath to do so baffled her. But if she could, she would rather not tell anyone here of her suspicions; she wanted to prove that she was more than a match for him. Or perhaps she wanted to give him the benefit of the doubt without exposing him to the attention of the British government and its employees. Whatever the cause, she wished more than anything that she didn't have to send Rupert out after Michael, but she knew that she had no choice.

Adolphus came to an abrupt halt in the shadows. "I am most disturbed, Elizabeth," he said sternly, "that you allowed that man to accost you. I am convinced you are unwell! Mama has some excellent medicines that have proved enormously helpful. Perhaps some of Bacon's Cordial Essence of Russia Rhubarb."

"I hardly think Essence of Russia Rhubarb will stop me from enjoying being kissed," Elizabeth said tartly, and then regretted it. Adolphus licked his lips, yanked her toward him with more force than she would have credited him, and proceeded to cover her face with wet, disagreeable kisses.

Elizabeth was outraged. More because he was polluting the earlier kiss that she had planned to dwell on at length when she was alone then for the actual damp salutations. "Stop it, Dolph!" she ordered, pushing against his corseted chest with ineffectual hands. "You forget yourself!"

He kept trying to reach her lips, but she managed to keep her face averted, noting absently how easy it was to avoid being kissed on the mouth if one really didn't care to be. His busy little hands were squeezing her, leaving damp stains on the satin, and she contemplated the rather rash extreme of treading on his instep, when a shadow loomed up and he was plucked off her like a struggling spider.

Adolphus thrashed about, his eyes bulging. "I say, Fraser, put me down this minute!" he squeaked. Michael Fraser held him for a moment longer, then dropped him roughly to the terrace. Adolphus staggered, his breathing even more labored, and the expression on his fat, pale face was frankly murderous.

"I'll see you cashiered for this," he said in a low, evil voice. "How dare you lay hands on me? I'm not without influence, you know, and I can have your head on a platter if I say the word."

"I doubt it," Fraser said briefly. "By all means try, if you care to. Though you're more likely to make a cake of yourself when it gets around that I was merely trying to protect a . . . what did you call Miss Traherne? A helpless flower of the female sex?"

"I would think my word would have better credit than yours," Adolphus said stiffly.

"No doubt. But you also happen to have a rather nasty scratch across your face that looks suspiciously like the marks from a lady's fingernails."

"And you'd no doubt back his word?" Adolphus demanded of Elizabeth sulkily.

"Without question."

"Trollop," he spat and found himself once more caught in Fraser's punishing grip.

"You will apologize to the *lady*," he ordered grimly, "or I will be forced to give you the beating you've deserved for years."

"I . . . I apologize," Adolphus gasped from his strangled throat, and Fraser released him abruptly. After a look of blind loathing, Sir Adolphus Wingert disappeared into the bushes, obviously in search of a more private entrance to Winfields. Fraser turned back to the shaken Elizabeth, and his expression was grim.

"You'd best get back to the jolly little party before your absence has been noticed by anyone other than the old witch.

And where in the world was your protective St. Ives while I was molesting you?"

"He must have thought he could trust you to behave like a gentleman," she said stiffly.

"Not Rupert. He knows me far too well," Fraser replied mysteriously. "Back to the house with you."

"Yes, Captain," she said meekly, determined to follow him the moment he took off into the bushes again.

As if reading her mind, he continued, "I'll be right behind you. And for God's sake, destroy that dress of yours when you retire tonight!"

"But why?"

"The British Empire is in trouble enough with the so-called Corsican monster plaguing our shores. The sight of you in that dress is enough to turn any red-blooded British soldier shatter-brained."

"Are you a red-blooded British soldier?" she inquired, thinking more in terms of politics than lust.

Fraser misread her question. "You know that I am," he replied shortly, turning her around with strong hands and giving her a little push in the direction of the drawing room doors. "And I would suggest you return to the drawing room before I prove it once again."

Elizabeth was sorely tempted, but for once she resisted. "You *will* be coming right in?"

"I told you that I would."

"Because if you decided not to," she continued inexorably, "I would be forced to ask Rupert to go outside and find you. Much as I would dislike taking such a rash action."

He stared at her for a long, silent moment. "I'm still more than a match for Rupert St. Ives." His voice was cold and still.

"I'm sure you are. I would prefer not to have to put it to test." Her eyes were beseeching in her set face, and Michael's grim expression lightened.

"I'll be right behind you," he said again in a softer tone. "Unless you'd rather stay out here with me for a while longer. We *were* interrupted."

Elizabeth's tense nerves relaxed, and she grinned up at him. "No, thank you, Captain," she said meekly, and reentered the warmth and light of the drawing room with only a faint feeling of regret.

Chapter 11

"WELL, THERE YOU are at last, Elizabeth," Lady Elfreda announced from across the room with her customarily piercing tones. "What in the world have you been doing out there in the garden on such a chilly night? You appear quite windblown."

Elizabeth put an absent hand to her hair, finding it comparatively sedate in its stern pinnings. She smiled sweetly at her nemesis. "The evening is quite delightful, Lady Elfreda. I am persuaded you would enjoy a brisk stroll almost as much as I did."

Her ladyship chose to ignore that suggestion. "Did you happen to see either Adolphus or Captain Fraser? They both disappeared around the time you decided to go for a walk."

The low hum of conversation had stopped by this time, and the small group of guests were no longer making any effort to conceal their interest. Rupert was eyeing her from one of the card tables with a particularly intimidating glower.

Elizabeth was irked. She simpered across the room at her ladyship, batting her eyes ingenuously. "Oh, la, your ladyship, it was monstrously exciting! There was I, merely seeking a breath of fresh air, when what should Captain Fraser do but leap out of the bushes, grab me, and kiss me quite fiercely. And then Dolph appeared, and threatened to knock Captain Fraser down, and started to escort me back to the house. But then Dolph tried to kiss me just as fiercely as Captain Fraser, and Captain Fraser appeared from out of the bushes and threatened to knock Dolph down, so I said—"

"You've said quiet enough already," Lady Elfreda snorted, much irritated. "Such a bunch of farradiddle I have never heard in my life."

"It comes from reading too many French novels,"

Elizabeth replied pertly, relief flooding her as she realized that Michael had entered the door directly behind her. "Why don't you ask Captain Fraser what the three of us were doing out there?"

Michael raised an inquiring eyebrow at the fascinated group. "Have you been divulging secrets, Miss Traherne?"

By this time Lady Elfreda appeared to have regretted the brouhaha she had instigated. "Well, I am certain that if both Dolph and Captain Fraser were present, then Miss Traherne was adequately chaperoned." She made a dismissing gesture with one claw-like hand, but Elizabeth chose to ignore her. She turned to Michael, smiling brilliantly.

"I was just telling them that both you and Dolph tried to kiss me and then decided to fight for my favors," she said impishly, daring him to refute it. Out of the corner of her eye she saw Rupert take a threatening step forward.

Fraser didn't bat an eye. "What a bouncer! And you a vicar's sister! The truth of the matter is, Lady Elfreda, that Miss Traherne came across Sir Adolphus and me blowing a cloud and threatened to cause a disturbance if we didn't allow her a puff of our cigars. Needless to say, we had no intention of complying with such blackmail, and she threatened to tell everyone that we molested her. Did you actually do so, Miss Traherne?" He said all this in his usual cool manner, but Elizabeth could see the amusement lingering in those blue eyes.

She bowed her head contritely to hide her own laughter. "I did," she said meekly, and Rupert's shoulders relaxed a trifle as he sat back down at the table.

"Elizabeth!" Sumner's scandalized voice caused her to start guiltily. "Are you lost to every vestige of propriety? How could you? When Sir Adolphus and Lady Elfreda have been everything that's kind?" Words failed him, and he stood there, his mouth opening and closing like a beached fish.

"I am wretchedly ungrateful," Elizabeth rejoined, agreeing sadly. "What can I do to make up for such outrageous behavior?"

Sumner had known his sister far too long to be taken in by

any show of contrition. His beautiful blue eyes were sharp as he scanned her demure face, and for the first time in twenty-four hours he forgot about the exotic contessa by his side. Before he could give his sister the sharp set down she so rightly deserved, Sir Henry Hatchett stepped smoothly into the breach.

"You could play cards with a boring old gentleman," he suggested in a fatherly tone. "Can't abide whist, never could. Much prefer piquet or silver loo. Why don't you do penance by keeping an old soldier entertained for a bit?"

A great harrumphing sound issued forth from General Wingert's pouter-pigeon chest. "I was about to suggest the same thing, Hatchett," he said, and there was a slight edge in his high-pitched voice and a glitter in his hot, dark little eyes.

Sir Henry smiled affably, taking Elizabeth's hand firmly in his own. "Then it's a great deal too bad that I beat you to it. However, your loss is my gain. Miss Traherne?" He gestured toward a deserted corner of the brightly lit ballroom.

She hesitated for a long moment General Wingert's portly face had turned a dark, angry red, and his thin mouth snapped shut. The pressure on Elizabeth's arm increased, and she gazed at Sir Henry with real relief, summoning her best smile for him. "I would be charmed, Sir Henry," she said in dulcet tones, her troubled gaze wandering over her shoulder to the general's retreating figure. There was something about Maurice Wingert that disturbed her, though she couldn't quite fathom what it was. It seemed far more dangerous than a touch of misplaced lechery.

She turned back to Sir Henry, temporarily banishing the worry from her mind. "You are most kind to ask me. Though I must say I consider that more of a reward than a punishment."

"You haven't played with him yet," Fraser said softly behind her so that no one else could hear. "Watch out he doesn't pinch you."

Elizabeth kicked backward, her heel connecting quite satisfactorily with Fraser's shin, before she moved gracefully across the room. Allowing herself a brief glance backward before she settled herself at a corner table, she was gratified to recognize an expression of pain around Fraser's dark blue eyes.

"What would you prefer to begin with, Miss Traherne? A hand or two of silver loo to start? Or would you prefer to go straight to piquet? Your brother tells me you are quite expert at it."

"My brother flatters me."

"Not too often, I would think. He appears to be a very disapproving young man," Sir Henry offered, shuffling with a practiced hand.

Elizabeth eyed him with open curiosity. He was an unassuming little man, with a balding pate surrounded by whimsical tufts of hair, a bulbous nose, grizzled eyebrows, and those surprisingly merry eyes. The white mustache drooped disconsolately, but Elizabeth was on her mettle. She was rapidly coming to the conclusion that Sir Henry was not the bumbling elderly gentleman he appeared to be.

"Why don't we start right off with piquet?" she suggested affably. "Though I must warn you that I am not allowed to gamble. Sumner considers it to be unbecoming in a vicar's sister, and I fear I am already in his black books as it is."

"Imaginary stakes, Miss Traherne?" he suggested. "A shilling a point?"

"Well, if they're going to be imaginary, I consider that paltry. A pound a point, at the very least."

"Done!" He dealt the cards rapidly. "I wonder if your clerical brother's reprobations apply to your brother Jeremy. A soldier can often spend far too much time gambling, much to his regret. Young Fraser there is a good example, I'm afraid."

Elizabeth took the bait. "He is?"

"Got himself into terrible debt over in Vienna, I heard. Gambling for outrageous stakes, and then the cards turned against him. There was some question of whether he might be able to pay up, but he came into some money unexpectedly."

"How?" Elizabeth had to ask, her heart sinking.

Sir Henry smiled genially. "Why, no one really knows. But fortunate for him, wouldn't you say? A gentleman always pays his gambling debts."

She could think of no reply to make, and the two quickly

became lost in the game. The only sounds were a mumbled "tierce, quart, not good, piquet" as they concentrated on the cards.

They were fairly well matched. Elizabeth had always prided herself on her playing, although she seldom had come up against a truly formidable player other than her brother Jeremy. Sir Henry was good but not extraordinary, and it required only a modicum of effort to keep pace with him. By the end of an hour's play Elizabeth held a slight lead—twenty mythical pounds—when Sir Henry abandoned his earlier silence.

"I have been hearing the most extraordinary tales, Miss Traherne," he began, his seemingly mild eyes astute beneath the grizzled eyebrows. "Lady Elfreda seems convinced that there is some sort of nefarious activity going on at Winfields this weekend. I wondered whether you might be able to enlighten me as to the particulars, or is this just an old lady's fancy?" He began the trick deviously, and Elizabeth almost allowed herself to be distracted by the card play to answer unguardedly.

"What does Lady Elfreda tell you, Sir Henry?" she questioned, concentrating on her unpromising hand.

"A great deal of nonsense, I'm sure. She's been suggesting that Michael Fraser is a French agent and that you are abetting him in his treasonous activities." This was all said in a bland tone of voice, but Elizabeth was not deceived. If anyone was behind the strange goings-on at Winfields, Sir Henry Hatchett was in the thick of it.

"Lady Elfreda," Elizabeth replied frankly, "has windmills in her head. She's so desperate not to lose her overgrown son that she would blacken anyone's good name."

"She sees you as a possible contender for Sir Aldophus's hand?" he questioned amiably.

"She has a great many foolish notions. As for Michael Fraser's loyalties, I am sure you would know a great deal more about that subject than I do."

"Why do you say that, Miss Traherne?"

"Because I know full well that you are in the intelligence section of the Foreign Office. I wouldn't be at all surprised if you and Rupert weren't here for the sole purpose of keeping an eye on that gentleman."

"Do you really think so?" There was a look of what Elizabeth might almost have called amusement on Sir Henry's cherubic countenance.

"I do." She discarded recklessly, intent on her purpose. "And I could be of immeasurable help to you if you would consider admitting me to your confidence. Is Michael Fraser a French agent?" She held her breath, scarcely daring to hear the answer.

She should have known Sir Henry was too cagy for her. "My dear, I haven't the faintest idea," he replied, taking her trick easily. "But I have a suggestion for you, if you would care to listen."

"I doubt I'll like it," she replied frankly, dealing with practiced ease.

"I doubt you will, but my conscience forces me to try. If there is anything going on here at Winfields this weekend, if Michael Fraser is not all he appears to be, then it would be extremely wise of you to keep out of the way. In my long career I have had some experience with French agents, and I may assure you that they are very dangerous fellows. Very dangerous, indeed. A foreign agent wouldn't think twice of wrapping that pretty hair around your throat and strangling you if you got in his way. Your brother Jeremy would tell you the same thing if he were here now."

"I only wish he was," she said sadly. "You think Michael would kill me?" The cards lay unattended on the table as her sherry-colored eyes met Hatchett's surprisingly acute ones.

"I would say, Miss Traherne, that you cannot be too careful."

"But what kind of answer is that?" she cried, both frightened and infuriated. "It appears obvious to me that you know precisely what is going on here, and yet you won't even tell me who I may safely trust."

"I have told you everything I am at liberty to tell," he said calmly.

"Which is exactly nothing."

"Except to be careful."

"Oh, pooh!" she said rudely. "I already knew that."

"It hardly seemed likely in the face of your recent behavior. It hasn't been that of a prudent young lady."

"Fustian!" retorted Elizabeth. "I can take care of myself."

"But that, my dear Miss Traherne, is precisely what I've been trying to tell you. You cannot take care of yourself when you haven't even the slightest idea what is going on."

"But—"

"The less you know, the better," he interjected repressively as he recognized the hopeful look on her mutinous face.

"You sound just like Sumner," she shot back.

"Do I really?" He appeared much struck. "Well, there's nothing that can be done about it. Does he have his advice dismissed as summarily as mine?"

"More summarily," she said, unabashed, eyeing her cards before declaring, "You are fairly in the way of being capotted, Sir Henry. You'd best look to your cards."

"I think, Miss Traherne, I must cry off. It's been a long day, and I am afraid I am completely out of my depth against your expertise. At least in the field of cards." He picked up his hand and frowned. "I say, Fraser," he said, raising his voice slightly. "Come here and play out this *partie*. This wench is fairly ruining me. She needs a younger man to sharpen her wits against."

Fraser moved across the room with an ostentatious and totally specious limp. "If Miss Traherne can bear with my company," he said in that slow, deep voice that had its customary enervating effect on her, "I would be more than happy to try to beat her at her own game. Though perhaps she'd prefer to play with St. Ives."

"No, you'll be fine," Hatchett said cheerfully, vacating his seat and bowing to a startled Elizabeth. "I've got to spirit young Rupert away with me, anyway. Don't let this young dog try and trick you, Miss Traherne. He's up to all sorts of devilment. You want to watch out for him."

"I will be more than careful, Sir Henry," she said in measured tones as Fraser sat down opposite her. "I shan't allow Captain Fraser to gammon me."

"Won't you, Lizzie?" he questioned softly when Sir Henry had moved out of hearing.

"Not likely. I intend to beat you roundly, at this game and any other you choose to play," she said with unaccustomed fierceness. "And why in the world are you limping? I didn't kick you that hard."

A slow smile lit his face. "I wanted to remind you of it," he said blandly, picking up Sir Henry's hand and staring at it with an absorbed air. "Tell me, what did the old man have to say? Did he warn you against me?"

"He did. Not that I needed any warning. I offered my services in trying to catch you, but he declined them, quite graciously, as a matter of fact."

A small frown creased the broad expanse of Fraser's forehead as he placed his discards face down on the table and drew from the major talon. "Did he really? And I suppose it is too much to hope that you decided to retire gracefully into the wings for the remainder of the weekend?"

"It is, indeed. If Sir Henry won't accept my help, then I shall have to continue on my own."

"Tell me, my dear Lizzie, what exactly do you hope to discover?"

"Whether or not you are an agent," she snapped. "Quint."

"Not good," he said dulcetly. "Octet. But why do you care whether or not I'm an agent?"

Elizabeth was silenced for only a moment. "Because of my brother, Jeremy," she said finally. "Anything a French agent does puts his life in danger. And anyone who endangers my brother had best beware of me."

"Why?" he inquired blandly. "What horrid vengeance would you wreak?"

"I, I would . . . ," she foundered, lost. "Oh, do be quiet. I cannot concentrate on this game."

With a nod Fraser did as she requested, but it was little help. In the first place, luck had favored him, and it took no time at all to prove that he was the far superior player, coolheaded where Elizabeth was rash, farseeing where Elizabeth went for the easy point. Two games were played, with Elizabeth going down rather badly.

"I fear I am outclassed," she said ruefully, counting up the points.

"You haven't had enough practice," he said negligently. "You're still rather young."

"I would hardly call three and twenty rather young," she shot back. "You need only ask Sumner to know how truly I am on the shelf."

"I wouldn't ask your brother a thing. Nor should you. If you're wondering how I managed to beat you quite so soundly, you may always content yourself with the knowledge that I supported myself through the army by playing cards with my fellow officers."

"So Sir Henry warned me."

"Did he really? Well, I am no Captain Sharp, if that is what you're thinking. I am merely quite good at piquet. I seldom play with flats."

"Are you suggesting that I am a flat?" she inquired in a dangerous tone of voice, her usually warm brown eyes quite cool.

"Never would I suggest such a thing! Although it was quite obvious to me in the garden that your experience has been rather limited."

Elizabeth felt the color suffuse her face. "You are quite right, sir. I am not in the habit of being kissed and manhandled. Someone of your expertise could no doubt easily tell that."

He nodded. "It was obvious. However, for an amateur you showed a surprising aptitude, both in kissing and being... manhandled. I am persuaded that you could become quite expert with very little practice."

She looked away from him in sudden confusion and found herself staring straight into General Wingert's unreadable dark eyes. She felt a sudden chill and forced her attention back to her partner, summoning up a belated anger. "How gratifying," she replied in icy tones. "And if I ever wish to acquire more experience, I will be certain to let you know."

A slow smile lit his tanned face, starting at the well-shaped sensual mouth that no longer seemed quite so grim and reaching the dark blue depths of his sapphire eyes. "I would appreciate that," he murmured. "I will endeavor to make myself available, unless, of course, you manage to have me convicted of spying. Do you know what the British do to traitors, Lizzie?" His voice was soft and enticing, but there was a bleak note of steel beneath it.

Her warm brown ryes met his. "I . . . I don't suppose I thought about it."

"They are executed, of course. In quite a nasty way, actually. I've seen it done, to my regret. You wouldn't like it, you know. And if you were instrumental in my conviction, I would think they would expect you to be there."

Elizabeth swallowed, her throat suddenly dry. "I have little doubt you would escape quite handily," she rallied, but the words were surprisingly hoarse.

"Oh, I think you underestimate the British Army. And I haven't a title to save me from a traitor's death. They would sever my limbs, my sweet Lizzie, while I still lived."

"Dear heavens," Elizabeth said faintly.

Fraser reached out and took one of her limp hands in his strong, warm one. "I am certain," he continued, "that you would at least have the satisfaction of knowing you had served your country. And I wouldn't think you'd mind having my blood on these lovely hands too terribly much, would you?" He lifted it up and placed his mouth against her palm, his lips seeming to burn her.

"You, you complete wretch!" she said shakily, snatching her hand away. "If you think you can cut a wheedle with me by frightening me—"

"Ask your dear, knowledgeable brother, Lizzie," he interjected in an affable voice. "Or ask Adolphus. They will tell you. They will also, if prompted, recount to you the tale of poor George Farrington, who was executed in '09 for treason. Two years later they found he was innocent. They cleared his name, but it wasn't much consolation to his family. The Crown does make mistakes sometimes."

"Don't!"

"Would you hold my hand, dear Lizzie, when the dread time comes?" he inquired softly. "Until, of course, they hack it off."

She pushed back the table hastily and ran from the room without a word. If she had chanced to look back, she would have been surprised by the most interesting expression on Michael Fraser's usually aloof face and an equally curious reaction from at least one other inhabitant of the ballroom.

Chapter 12

ELIZABETH DID NOT sleep well that night. With Captain Fraser's horrid vision still ripe in her mind, she had bid a hasty good night to Lady Elfreda and the glowering Adolphus. The ministrations of his excellent valet had managed to remove all signs of rough handling from his pale pink toilette, and only the sullen pout on the moon face told anyone of the contretemps in the garden. The protruding blue eyes were politely hostile, and Elizabeth felt a pang of regret that she had antagonized what was basically a very pleasant fellow. She gave him her best smile and was rewarded with a coolly distant nod.

Better than a leer and a pinch, she thought resignedly. She would have liked to ask Rupert if a traitor's fate was truly so hideous. But he was nowhere in sight, and so she made her solitary way to her bedroom, feeling rejected and slightly sorry for herself. Rupert had abandoned her, and Captain Fraser, apart from his horrifying and no doubt completely fanciful tales of severed limbs, hadn't made the slightest effort to keep her at the table. Granted, she had run so fast that he hadn't had much of a chance to stop her, but she felt unreasonably that he should have tried. Doubtless he had just sat there, watching her departure out of those disturbing blue eyes, with no expression at all on the smooth planes of his tanned, handsome face.

Well, it was patently absurd, she told herself as she wrestled with her clothing. As if His Majesty's government would behave so odiously even to traitors! It would make them little better than the monsters of the French Revolution with their infamous guillotine. Not that some of the French aristocracy hadn't deserved it, she added with a libertarian air.

And not that a French agent who was busily engaged in selling out his own country to the Corsican monster didn't deserve it, she added gloomily, yanking at her laces and remembering with a blush her assistant of the night before. She could almost imagine those cool, deft hands on her skin, and a small, helpless moan escaped her. Drat the man!

Her dreams were far from pleasant that night. She found herself strolling casually through a snowy field, though the temperature was quite warm, and she was dressed in her shift and petticoats, barefoot, with her chestnut hair hanging like a curtain down her back. Sumner was standing to one side, a disapproving expression on his pale, handsome face as he quoted some of Saint Paul's more sour reproaches, and Brenna, dressed as a nun, shook her head sadly. At the far end of the field was Michael Fraser, too far away for her to read his expression. She knew she had to reach him before it was too late, but Adolphus and Rupert seemed determined to stop her.

"But you cannot go to him," said Rupert with great practicality. "He has no feet."

The dream Elizabeth paid no attention, pushing him out of her way and running the seemingly interminable distance across the field. Flinging herself in Michael's waiting arms, she held on as tightly as she could. Looking up into his eyes, she recognized the expression of rueful amusement.

"You're far too late, Lizzie," he said mildly. "They've already killed me." And she knew that if she looked down, his feet would be gone. She opened her mouth to scream. . . .

She sat bolt upright in her bed, her skin crawling with remembered horror, tears not far from her frightened eyes. It was pitch-black in her cavernous bedroom. The fire had burned to a mere glow of embers, and the moon had already set, leaving a dark, cloudy sky outside the tall, leaded-glass windows.

With great determination Elizabeth lay down again, trying to will herself back to sleep. It was to no avail. Every time she closed her eyes, she pictured Fraser's dismembered body, his beautiful eyes staring up at her beseechingly. Sighing, she sat up again, struggling with a tinder to light her bedside candle. There was no question of sleep right now. She had finished her novel, and the great house was quiet, the various inhabitants sleeping the sleep of the just or the conscienceless, she couldn't be sure which.

It is now or never, Lizzie, she told herself firmly, using the pet name deliberately. After all, it was a very nice sort of name, even if it came from a spy and a traitor. If you're going to find that list, you certainly couldn't choose a better time. The entire house is asleep. No sober voice answered her, telling her not to be foolish, to blow out the candle and go back to sleep. There was only the silence of the sleeping house.

Sighing, she pulled herself out of bed. A little predawn stroll to the deserted battlements to prove her suspicions unfounded and then she could sleep for hours. Thank heavens she wouldn't have to rise early for one of Sumner's tedious Sunday services. Or would she?

Wrapping a frilly lace robe around her tall, well-rounded body, she picked up the candle and opened the door. Without a sound, she slipped out and shut the door behind her. Maybe a detour by way of the library and the brandy bottle wouldn't be amiss.

The rattle of a doorknob alerted her. Blowing out the candle, she slipped down behind a large upholstered chair, scarcely daring to breath. A door opened, a candle glow illuminated the hallway, and the elegant figure of the contessa, scantily clad in black lace and ribbons, emerged. Elizabeth noted with interest that she had made her exit from Sir Maurice's bedroom. Peering about nervously, the contessa tiptoed down the hall, scratched on the door, and entered. Elizabeth was frozen with shock and fury. It was Michael's door!

She crouched there, her mind ablaze with rage and speculation. Before she could order her thoughts, however, another doorknob turned. She cast a surreptitious glance toward Michael's door, but this time she was astounded to see her brother, clad gloriously in purple flannel, his golden locks freshly brushed, move swiftly down the hallway toward the rooms originally allotted to the contessa. With a muffled knock, he turned the handle and entered, shutting the door behind him.

She's not there, Elizabeth thought grimly. She's busy with

him. The door beside her opened again, and the contessa stepped out, moving past Elizabeth's crouching figure with a heavy trail of musk-scented perfume. She went straight into Sir Henry's bedroom, this time without so much as a knock. It was little wonder Lady Beatrice found herself indisposed this weekend.

Sumner stepped out of the contessa's rooms, a petulant expression on his handsome, immature face, and moved swiftly back to his own rooms. He disappeared into them just in time, as Adolphus's mountainous form, clad in a dressing gown of a truly ominous Paisley, with twelve frogs down his massive front, appeared from around the corner. The door next to Elizabeth's crouched body opened, and Michael stepped out, saw Adolphus's approaching form, and to Elizabeth's surprise strode on silent, bare feet to meet his host. He was still dressed, albeit in shirt-sleeves, and it was no effort on Elizabeth's part to compare the two dissimilar men. Michael won by a wide margin.

"There you are!" Adolphus cried in a disgruntled voice. "I was expecting to hear from someone tonight. I must say I don't care to be left in the dark this way. It's as much my business as anyone else's. After all, the papers were hidden in *my* house." He sounded like nothing so much as a spoiled child. "I think I have a right to know."

"We've told you everything we can, Sir Adolphus," Michael said soothingly, and Elizabeth knew immediately that he was lying. "As soon as we're able to find out where the information was hidden—"

"How do I know I can trust you? You've got a damned shady reputation, Fraser."

"I thought you found my credentials acceptable," he replied mildly enough, and Elizabeth craned her neck to hear Adolphus's mumbled reply.

"Well, if (the name was unintelligible) says so, I suppose I have no choice but to accept it. But I must warn you away from Miss Traherne. She's a veritable innocent, hasn't been out in the world much, and she's likely to have her head turned by a fellow of your address. I must ask you to leave her alone. I'd think you'd be too busy to get up a flirtation with an aging spinster."

Fraser laughed. "I would scarcely call Miss Traherne an aging spinster, Sir Adolphus. And if that's how you view her, I'm surprised you find it necessary to defend her. Her brothers would certainly be the ones to demand to know my intentions."

"Miss Traherne is a connection of mine. I feel, as head of the family—"

"You'd like a bit of slap and tickle yourself, Sir Adolphus," Michael concluded bluntly. "You may rest assured that Miss Traherne stands in no danger of ravishment from me."

"Well, I would hardly have thought so. She isn't quite your style, is she?" Adolphus said smugly.

"Oh, now, I wouldn't say that," Michael responded lazily. "I merely have other things on my mind right now." He made a dismissing gesture. "Go back to bed, Sir Adolphus. I am not, as you obviously suspect, about to sneak into Miss Traherne's bedroom and have my wicked way with her. I prefer my women willing. As soon as I find out anything more about the papers, I will inform you. I am sure you can be trusted." The irony in his voice was heavy, but Adolphus, not being precisely needle-witted, appeared to take his words at face value.

"Very well. And I suppose I'll have to trust *you*. I haven't any choice in the matter. But I must remind you that my mother has a frail constitution. I don't want anything to upset her."

"Your mother is a Valkyrie," Fraser said bluntly. "She'd stand up to blood and gore far better than most soldiers would, I make no doubt. Good evening, Sir Adolphus." Without another word he disappeared back into his room, shutting the door behind him with a decided snap.

Elizabeth crouched there, her mind awhirl. Why in the world would Adolphus, the proud and honorable sixth baron Wingert, allow a mere captain in the service of his aging uncle to speak so disrespectfully to him? And exactly what was going on? Was Adolphus a traitor too? Or had the diabolically clever Captain Fraser succeeded in pulling the wool over his eyes? Or was Captain Fraser not the blackguard he seemed?

That was almost too much to hope for, and Elizabeth felt as if she must scream from uncertainty and frustration. She knew she would gladly give ten years off her life to find out whether she could trust the man, and she felt even more determined to discover exactly what was going on.

Adolphus still stood in the middle of the hallway, obviously undecided as to his next move. He stared back at the shut doors around him meditatively.

The door to Elizabeth's other side opened, and the contessa was once more in the hallway. Without a word she slithered up to Adolphus, threading her slender arm through his burly one, and led him, like a master leading his prize pig, down the hall to her bedroom.

Sumner's door opened as they went past and then silently closed, an eloquent expression of doomed love and disappointment. Finally Adolphus and his friend were out of sight, and Elizabeth was just about to stretch her cramped muscles, when Fraser's door opened one more time.

"Go back to bed, Lizzie," he said in even tones, and shut the door again before she had time to do anything more than gasp in outrage as she struggled to her feet.

"Damn," she muttered, and retired obediently to her room, not even bothering to lock the door. If she tried to make it to the tower, she had little doubt Fraser would follow her. The moment her head hit the pillow, she was asleep again, although this time her dreams were a great deal more pleasant, if markedly more licentious.

Chapter 13

Sunday

ELIZABETH OPENED her eyes suddenly as a small, almost inaudible sound penetrated the heavy mists of sleep. She lay there in the soft, warm bed, every nerve atingle, her heart thudding, her palms damp. Then she placed the noise. It had been the unmistakable click of her heavy oak door shutting. But had it been shutting someone in or out?

Slowly, imperceptibly, she moved her head a fraction of an inch, peering through half-closed eyes. In the early morning light her room was blessedly deserted. Swinging herself out of bed with a sudden upsurge of energy, Elizabeth dashed to the door on icy bare feet, hesitating only a moment before flinging it open to peer down the long, dim hallway. Not a soul in sight, of course, she thought bitterly, shutting the door behind her and padding back toward the cold ashes of last night's fire. And in this inhospitable house she could scarcely console herself with the reflection that it had merely been a chambermaid seeing to her comfort by bringing early morning tea or reviving her fire. Thanks to Lady Elfreda, no doubt abetted by Brenna, no such amenities were offered Miss Elizabeth Traherne. If she wanted a little warmth and something hot to drink (preferably Mrs. Kingpin's coffee), she would have to find it herself, despite the early hour and her foreshortened night's sleep.

When Jeremy had left, he had entrusted the gold-chased pocket watch that their father had bequeathed him into her care. Sumner had done his best to filch it from her, proclaiming that he had more right to it than she did and that old Jeremy must have preferred him to have it. But Elizabeth had remained steadfast, either keeping it on her person or hiding it from Sumner's acquisitive fingers. Pulling it out from between the mattresses, she gave a small groan. Six forty-five. She looked back at the bed longingly and then squared her shoulders. If she was to be of any use at all, she couldn't succumb to the pleasures of the flesh, the most enticing of which right now was her bed. She had been balked of her chance to search for the list last night. Considering everyone's nocturnal activities, she ought to be fairly certain they would all sleep late, and she could wander about this rabbit's warren to her heart's content without running into anyone more sinister than a sleepy scullery maid or two.

Dressing more for warmth and practicality than beauty in a round gown of soft green kerseymere, she performed a sketchy toilette, splashing cool water over her face and running a brush through her hair before pinning it back haphazardly with a few silver hairpins. There would be no one to impress at this hour of the morning, she assured herself, closing the door behind her with a silent click, the click reminding her of the noise that had first awakened her out of her sound sleep. Unless she ran into her early morning visitor, she thought, suddenly uneasy. She looked back toward her bedroom with longing and then shook herself. She had to do her best. If Jeremy could risk his life for her safety, could be lying dead or wounded in some French battlefield at this very moment, she could at least . . . at least. . . .

Her thoughts faltered as the face of the drowned French spy returned with horrid clarity. She might be found down at Starfield Cove in the same condition, and who knew whose hands would send her. Michael Fraser's? The thought was almost too much to bear. The mysteriously familiar figure of Mr. Fredericks down at the beach was a far more acceptable choice for the role of villain and murderer. Surely there was something sinister in the set of his shoulders, something inherently evil in his stance? The eerie familiarity only added to Elizabeth's sense of impending danger.

"Well, Miss Elizabeth, I wasn't expecting to see you so early this morning," Mrs. Kingpin announced, placing a thick, steaming mug of coffee in front of her. "I would have thought you and Miss O'Shea would have slept late on such a day, especially after all the dancing and jollity of last night."

"Brenna's up?" Elizabeth questioned, taking a deep drink and burning her tongue.

"She was sitting here in the kitchen when I got up, just staring into the fire, poor thing. I think she's suffered a disappointment in love," Mrs. Kingpin confided, her many chins wobbling dolefully. "She wouldn't touch a bit of food and just wandered off looking like a lost soul, poor wee thing."

"Poor wee thing," Elizabeth echoed absently, taking a more cautious sip of coffee. "Did you happen to see which direction she went?"

Mrs. Kingpin shook her iron-gray head. "I was far too busy, Miss Elizabeth. I would expect she's in the library or wandering out in the front gardens."

"Then I'll head for the back gardens," Elizabeth announced, taking her mug and heading toward the door. "I am feeling equally somber, and I don't feel much like a conversation with Miss Brenna O'Shea. She's not the friendliest of companions in the best of circumstances, and I don't doubt she'll be positively deadly this morning."

Despite her words, Elizabeth made straight for the library. Even running into Brenna was worth the risk. What better place to hide an important paper than among other, innocuous papers? There must be a thousand places in the library to hide a purloined list of spies, and it was definitely a far more pleasant place to search before braving the rigors of the east tower. Elizabeth was not overly fond of heights.

Despite her hopes, she was doomed to deep disappointment. Adolphus obviously spent the bare minimum of time in the loftily proportioned room that served as a library. The elegant Louis Quatorze desk was bare of papers, the drawers were empty, and the shelves and shelves of hand-tooled leather books were coated with a film of dust that hailed from well more than a month ago, when the French spy had met his untimely end. Brenna was scarcely the housekeeper Lady Elfreda touted her as being, and the Wingerts were as ill-read as Elizabeth suspected. So much for this avenue of endeavor, she thought, closing the door behind her and heading toward the back gardens. Michael Fraser had been out there for a reason; perhaps in the calm morning light she could find some proof of his eventual destination. If worse came to worst, a stroll up the east tower might become a necessity. For Jeremy's sake, she reminded her flagging spirits sternly.

The air was damp and cool in the garden, the dew still fresh on the budding philodendrons, the neat little pathways wet beneath her slippered feet. It was going to be a beautiful day, unseasonably warm, and Elizabeth decided to allow herself a brief moment of peace before she continued her investigations. The marble bench glistened in the early sunlight, and Elizabeth sat, sipping at the now lukewarm coffee and staring meditatively into the bushes.

"I didn't expect to see you up and about so early," an endearingly familiar voice drawled in her ear, surprisingly close. Fraser's hand dropped lightly to her shoulder, and it was with a great effort that Elizabeth controlled her nervous start as she turned to look up at him.

"Damn and blast," she said distinctively, making no move to shake off his hand. "I hadn't expected to see you, either, after all your visitors last night."

He smiled seraphically and dropped down on the marble bench beside her, filching the mug of coffee with one deft hand. "Why is it such a great disappointment, my love? Were you expecting someone else at this ungodly hour? The noble Captain St. Ives perhaps?" He took a swallow of her coffee, and a pained expression clouded his dark blue eyes. "What in God's name is this wretched stuff?" he demanded weakly.

"Cold coffee. And I am not your love, Captain Fraser. Nor am I Rupert St. Ives's love, either, for that matter. Not that it's any of your concern. I merely wished for a bit of solitude on this lovely spring morning. I find the atmosphere at Winfields a trifle oppressive."

"Not without reason," Michael replied, putting the mug down with a lingering shudder and possessing himself of one of Elizabeth's not unwilling hands. "But do you know, I do not feel the slightest bit oppressed at this moment."

Elizabeth felt a treacherous melting inside her, a melting she knew was far too dangerous, and just what the devious Captain Fraser had in mind.

"Do you not?" she inquired in dulcet tones, snatching her hand away and drawing herself up. "Then I trust you'll enjoy yourself even more if I leave you alone. I find I have a sudden need for solitude."

She turned to leave him, intent on running as fast and as far from temptation as possible, when his hand shot out and caught her wrist, dragging her up against his strong, lean body as his other arm snaked around and imprisoned her.

"Solitude is the last thing I had in mind, Lizzie," he whispered in her ear. "And besides, I know perfectly well that if I were to leave you alone, you would be bound to stick your pretty little nose exactly where it doesn't belong. A place that could bring great danger both to yourself and to me. So you see"—his mouth came hypnotizingly closer to her breathlessly parted lips—"I have no intention of letting you go."

He made no move to kiss her, seeming content to let his mouth hover tantalizingly as his eyes bore into hers, an unreadable expression in their dark blue depths. Elizabeth knew she should offer some token resistance, a resistance she found curiously hard to summon.

"Michael," she said, as his hand reached up and deftly stripped the silver pins out of her hair, letting the waves tumble down her back. "You shouldn't—"

He didn't bother letting her finish the sentence. That tantalizing mouth hovered no longer but swooped down on her like a bird of prey, plundering her soft lips ruthlessly. With a small sigh of despair, Elizabeth slid her arms around his neck and closed her eyes, surrendering to the small death of his kiss.

He moved his mouth a fraction away, letting his lips brush against her closed eyelids, her cheeks, her trembling lips once more, as his strong arms pressed her soft curves closer against the muscular hardness of his body. Elizabeth was shaking from head to toe, and it was with an awed fascination that she realized he was shaking, too.

"Lizzie," he murmured against the scented waves of her hair, and his voice was hoarse. "Lizzie, you must listen to me. It's dangerous."

At that precise moment a noise came to their ears, an unmistakable groan. Fraser stiffened, his body rigid, and Elizabeth, with belated good sense, ripped herself out of his arms.

"What was that?"

"It sounded unpleasantly like a groan," Fraser replied dryly. As if in confirmation, another moan issued forth, and Elizabeth took off in the direction of the cry.

"Damn it, Lizzie," Fraser cursed, and followed her into the bushes. "Have you got no sense whatsoever?"

Whatever Elizabeth expected to find, it certainly wasn't Brenna O'Shea sitting in an awkward little heap, her face unnaturally pale, her hand to her tousled head. Elizabeth flew to her side. "Brenna, are you all right?"

Brenna looked up with her customary cool dislike in her green eyes. "Of course I'm not, Elizabeth," she said crossly. "I must have had a fainting spell. My poor head hurts abominably, my dress is grass-stained, and I dislike above all things people making fusses over me."

"I gather you'll survive," Elizabeth observed dryly. "What happened?"

Brenna's eyes flew upward as Fraser appeared on the scene, and the look she cast Elizabeth was decidedly speculative. "I don't precisely remember. I was simply taking the air, when suddenly everything went blank. I found myself lying here with a beastly headache and not the vaguest idea how I got here. Last thing I remember, I was wandering by the east tower. I suppose it was a fainting spell, but I am not accustomed to them."

"You've been under a great deal of strain recently," Elizabeth offered tentatively, and was rewarded with a look of deep scorn from Brenna's sharp eyes.

"I am not the type to faint from a broken heart, Elizabeth," she observed tartly. "Your hand, Captain Fraser," she requested, her voice softening into a beguiling little tone that set Elizabeth's teeth on edge.

Michael complied swiftly, a troubled expression on his face. "You say you were walking by the east tower, Miss O'Shea?"

"That's where I usually walk. I have little doubt this dizzy spell comes from not enough sleep and infrequent meals," Brenna said, smiling wanly at the captain while she ignored the fuming Elizabeth. "I shall feel more the thing once I lie down on my bed for a bit."

"I'll accompany you back to the house," Fraser offered swiftly, and Elizabeth controlled a strong desire to kick him again. She should have slapped his face when she had the chance instead of melting into his arms like a perfect ninnyhammer.

"There's no need, Captain. I prefer to go on my own. Besides, I've already interfered too much in your little assignation. Good morning, Elizabeth," she added, and moved off toward the house with only a trace less than her usual grace.

Once she was out of earshot, Elizabeth rounded on Michael. "She had a bump on her head the size of an egg," she said abruptly. "She may think she fainted, but I am convinced she was attacked."

"No doubt," Fraser said in a distracted tone of voice, his eyes staring off in the distance, directly at the east tower.

Elizabeth's irritation flared. "And you probably were the one who did it," she snapped, all caution thrown to the wind. "You probably found her prowling around the east tower and clubbed her on the head so she wouldn't discover exactly what you're up to, and then you sneak up on me all smiles and flattery, thinking I would fall for it."

This caught his attention. "And did you?" he inquired sweetly. "Fall for my evil stratagems, that is?"

Excuse enough, Elizabeth decided, and slapped him across the face. "Not for a moment."

He didn't even blink, and the faint smile never left his face. "How very devious you are, Lizzie. You had me quite persuaded otherwise."

"Damn you, Fraser!"

"*Tsk, tsk.* Such language from a vicar's sister," he chided.

"I'm a soldier's sister also," she shot back.

"You don't mean to try to convince me that Jeremy taught you to swear like that?" he inquired incredulously. "I wouldn't have thought it of him."

There was a sudden, deathly silence in the garden, broken only by the early morning cry of the larks. "You know Jeremy?" she asked, and her voice was quiet.

A frown had creased Fraser's brow, and to Elizabeth's observant eyes he seemed irritated with himself. "I've met him," he said briefly. "But that's not what we were discussing."

"That's what I was discussing," she shot back. "That is what I wish to discuss. Where did you meet Jeremy? Have you seen him recently? Oh, Michael, is he all right?"

"As far as I know, your brother is enjoying his customary good health," Fraser said stiffly. "I'm far more interested in what caused that lump on Miss O'Shea's head than whatever is occupying your ramshackle brother."

"Ramshackle?" Elizabeth fumed.

"With a definite resemblance to his ramshackle sister," Fraser added deftly. It crossed Elizabeth's mind that he was being deliberately provoking, but she didn't care. She drew back to slap his mocking face again, but she found her wrist caught in a numbing grip.

"You may slap me once, dearest Lizzie, but twice I will not allow. I am very likely to hit back at that point."

"You wouldn't dare," she breathed, outraged.

"Try me, Lizzie," he drawled.

Wrenching her arm free, she gave him her fiercest glare, a look of extreme loathing that left him more amused than moved.

"That's right, my love. I would suggest you avoid me at all costs and hate me to your heart's content. I am a very dangerous fellow, you know. And I'm afraid I don't have time for you right now, much as I wish I did." His eyes lingered suggestively on Elizabeth's mouth.

There was no way she could control the blush that rose in her face at the deliberate reminder of how completely she'd surrendered to his kiss, and there was no way she could control the fury that raced through her.

"Even General Wingert is more of a gentleman than you," she shot back.

"Very likely," he agreed amiably. "I suggest you seek him out."

"Perhaps I shall," Elizabeth said, suddenly struck. "He may be more forthcoming than you are."

"I would sincerely doubt it, Lizzie. But by all means try," he offered. "I only trust you won't regret it. The general's reputation with the fair sex is unsavory, to say the least. And this time I won't be there to rescue you."

She struggled for a parting retort, but her mind remained a stubborn blank. She knew far too well that he was right, and she also knew that what she really wanted was to throw herself back into his arms—curse the dratted man! Without another word she flounced out of the garden, leaving him to his nefarious activities. Perhaps Rupert could stop him.

Chapter 14

WHEN ELIZABETH entered the breakfast salon two hours later and saw the solitary bewigged figure of Lady Elfreda at the head of the table, she started to beat a hasty retreat. She had spent an unpleasant two hours fuming in her room, and Lady Elfreda was the last person Elizabeth felt like indulging in a tête-à-tête. Unfortunately, her hostess's eyes were eagle-sharp, and she had been lying in wait for her prey that morning.

"Where do you think you're going, Elizabeth?" she demanded.

"I ... I forgot my reticule," Elizabeth replied, struggling lamely for an excuse.

"You won't need it at breakfast; I have no intention of charging you for the meal. Serve yourself and sit down beside me. We haven't had a chance for a comfortable coze this weekend." This invitation was accompanied by a hideous smile showing all of Lady Elfreda's overlarge teeth, a crocodile smile if ever there was one, but Elizabeth was nothing if not brave.

Filling her plate sparingly, she took her seat with a cautious air. Lady Elfreda was not to be trusted. "Where are the others?" she inquired politely, applying herself to her morning coffee.

"They've all scattered to the four winds. Except for Brenna, who is behaving like an invalid, complaining of a headache caused, no doubt, by a broken heart. Why in the world she should set her heart on your beautiful, dimwitted brother is beyond my comprehension."

It was beyond Elizabeth, too, but illogically she jumped to Sumner's defense. "My brother is very kind, very good, and very, very handsome. Brenna could count herself lucky to marry him."

"Your brother is a beautiful bore," her ladyship said frankly. "Not that I object. I think that all ministers should be beautiful and boring. It suits 'em. But they're not my idea of entertaining company. You, for all your faults, ain't boring," she conceded handsomely.

"Thank you very much," Elizabeth replied in cool tones. "And I must say I hardly find your ladyship boring either."

Lady Elfreda's heavy jaw snapped shut, and she eyed her impertinent guest with an icy glare. "I did not arrange this so that we should argue, Elizabeth," she said in heavy tones.

"No? Then why did you arrange this?"

"To warn you. I feel it my duty, as the only sensible female of your acquaintance, and in some distant manner a connection, to warn you about Captain Fraser."

Elizabeth's hackles, already alert, rose. Taking a deliberately casual sip out of her hot, sweet coffee, she smiled encouragingly at her hostess. "What about Captain Fraser?"

"An alliance between your family and a man of Fraser's stamp would be very unfortunate, dear Elizabeth. Not that I think it would ever come to that point. But I've seen the way your eyes follow him around the room when you think he isn't looking. It really isn't the thing, Elizabeth, to throw yourself so blatantly at a man."

"I have not!" she said hotly. "As a matter of fact, I find him completely insupportable. He is rude, overbearing, arrogant, and completely odious."

"And you stare at him like a perfect moonling when you think no one is looking," Lady Elfreda snapped. "It's no wonder the man responds. Apart from the fact that he's scarcely been allowed near a properly bred young lady in the last several years. And to top it all off, you bear a striking resemblance to that unhappy girl he married."

"Married?" Elizabeth echoed in faint tones.

"Marianne Kimball. Dolph knew her rather well, I believe. She died in childbirth while he was off in the Peninsula. I believe it was quite a blow to poor Fraser."

"I hadn't realized he was a widower," Elizabeth said slowly, her mind sifting through this latest and unwelcome information.

"I'm surprised Dolph didn't tell you. Or that you strongly

resemble the poor girl."

"Perhaps I should ask him."

"Don't do that!" her ladyship ordered sternly. "It would upset him too much. He knew her quite well and felt she was treated rather badly. I'm afraid he holds it against Fraser."

Elizabeth looked at the plate in front of her and felt quite ill. The eggs tasted like dust in her mouth, and the coffee was cold.

"I thought you should be warned, Elizabeth," Lady Elfreda continued in a kindly tone. "I would consider myself derelict in my duty to allow you to go on imagining anything might come of this infatuation."

"There is no infatuation!" Elizabeth said sharply.

"Well, I'm glad to hear it. In the meantime, I wonder if you might do me a favor. Captain Fraser has gone for a brief ride before morning services."

"Morning services?" Elizabeth echoed uneasily.

"Your brother has consented to give us an informal talk on the scriptures this morning."

"Oh, God."

"Exactly." The old lady nodded her wig benevolently. "But I'm afraid Captain. Fraser ran off with my book of sermons. I had promised to show them to your brother before the services this morning. I do so hate to let him down. Would you be a dear and go fetch it? It should be right by his bed; he told me earlier that he read them before he retired. Not that I believe a miscreant like him. But I'm sure the book will be in plain sight, and you wouldn't run into anyone but the maid."

It was on the tip of Elizabeth's tongue to refuse outright, suggest that Brenna could do her ladyship's errands, or suggest that her ladyship go jump in the sea. But her common sense took over as she realized she would at last have a chance to look about Fraser's room for any sign of espionage or deceit. With proof, she could go to Rupert, lay the evidence before him, and beg for mercy. If Fraser could simply be made harmless, Jeremy and his like would be safe. And Fraser could escape to some place where he could do no damage.

"Certainly," she said affably, pushing away her plate and rising. "A book of sermons, did you say?"

"There shouldn't be more than one by the good captain's bed. Take your time, my dear. We'll all meet in the chapel in another hour."

The hall was deserted as Elizabeth made her way back toward her bedroom. The hidden paper could as easily be in Fraser's room as anywhere else. While he was out riding, she could search through his possessions with no one the wiser.

Fraser's bedroom was slightly smaller than Elizabeth's, with a massive oak bed that was a twin to hers, a less attractive view of the countryside, and an anteroom leading off to one side. The door was open, and for a moment Elizabeth thought she heard a noise within.

Absurd, she told herself sternly, shutting his door quietly behind herself and moving on silent feet into the room.

There was no book of sermons on the bedside table or anywhere in sight. All the drawers were empty, and she was halfway through the meager but elegant contents of the wardrobe when a noise directly behind her made her whirl around.

"Would it be impolite to inquire exactly what you are doing?" Fraser's deep, slow voice was amiable. "Not that I'm not enchanted to have you seek out my bedroom, but in the circumstances I could have wished you'd picked a better time for it."

Elizabeth's tawny skin turned pale and then deep red as she faced the room's inhabitant. He had obviously just stepped out of the bath, for he stood there clad in nothing but a towel knotted around his trim waist, his dark hair dripping onto his shoulders, his broad, tanned chest glistening with drops of water.

Elizabeth stared at that chest in fascination. The only other male chests she had seen unclothed were her brothers' when they were much, much younger, and without question Michael Fraser's made an admirable contrast.

"Well?" he questioned, as the silence lengthened. "Are you going to tell me why you're here? Not, I presume, to accost me in my bath."

"Lady Elfreda asked me to retrieve a book of sermons she lent you," Elizabeth stammered after a long moment.

Fraser's snort was derisive as he took a step closer. "Surely you can think of a better excuse than that! I'm not a complete flat, you know. Doubtless you thought I'd be out and abroad at this hour and decided to ignore all my previous warnings and scrabble through my clothes in search of heaven knows what. It's not here, you know."

All amiability was gone, and his voice was icy. The dark blue eyes that had been so lazily flattering a few hours earlier were now furious as they bored into her. Instinctively Elizabeth quailed before such unbridled anger, taking an involuntary step backward and nearly falling into the closet.

"It would serve you right," he continued in a dangerous voice, "if I told you exactly what was going on here. You don't seem to have any notion of how dangerous this entire situation is, or if you do, you simply don't care. That could have been you clubbed on the head this morning, instead of Brenna. You're not only risking your own life with your insatiable snooping, but you're also endangering me, your hosts, your family, and the security of this nation."

"Well!" Elizabeth said weakly. "You certainly don't try to minimize the situation."

"I ought to lock you in that closet," he said between clenched teeth, "and not let you out till Monday morning. Then perhaps you might learn some sense."

"My brother would be bound to miss me," she replied. "He's got a sermon all planned for his unsuspecting fellow guests, and if I'm not sitting there to frown at him, he'll go on for at least three hours."

Fraser stared at her for a long moment, and she met his gaze bravely, her face still pink from embarrassment. If only he were fully dressed. It was amazingly difficult to keep her gaze from wandering downward to his broad, bare chest. And the long, bare legs weren't bad, either.

After a moment he sighed. "I wonder what in the world I should do with you, Lizzie."

"Why, nothing at all," she replied brightly. "And now I'm late for chapel, and so are you. Lady Elfreda will be waiting for me." She sidled nervously toward the door.

Fraser let out a shout of laughter. "You needn't look so panicky, Lizzie. I am not about to throw you down on the bed and ravish you. The thought of your brother's disapproving sermon quite unmans me."

"I wasn't worried," she said with chilly dignity.

"Though if I thought it would keep you out of trouble, I'd be tempted."

Elizabeth's hot temper flared. "Of course that would be the only reason why you could possibly want to," she shot back. "Well, don't worry, Captain. You won't be forced into seducing such a veritable antidote. After all, you've sacrificed so much for your country already." She stormed toward the door, with Fraser just behind her.

"Lizzie," he said, vastly amused, "don't be absurd. You know there's nothing I'd like better than to—"

He had just managed to grab her arm, pulling her back against him, when the door was flung open. Standing there like an avenging angel was Adolphus, this time attired in pale lavender, with Lady Elfreda and Rupert St. Ives directly behind him.

It was a colorful tableau: Elizabeth, her cheeks flushed and eyes shining with rage, Fraser in his towel with his arm around her, and Adolphus staring at the two of them in horror as Lady Elfreda, an expression of malicious triumph on her raddled face, looked on with ill-concealed delight.

But it was Rupert who took the offensive, his normally tanned face pale with rage. "What is the meaning of this, Fraser? Take your hands off Miss Traherne at once!" he thundered, before Adolphus could do more than stare, gasping for breath like a landed perch.

Fraser released her arm with deliberate, insolent leisureliness. The anger in the air was like electricity, and the danger was very real. The two men were hard, implacable enemies, and she had somehow put herself in the middle of them, giving them the excuse they so badly wanted to kill each other.

She reached out and threaded her arm through Rupert's uniform-clad one, feeling the muscles bunched in fury beneath her hand. She knew perfectly well that Lady Elfreda would deny the errand that had sent her into such a contretemps, and her fertile brain was working feverishly.

"Don't be absurd, Rupert," she said with an airy laugh. "It's my fault entirely. I was rushing around, trying to get ready for the service, and I stumbled into the wrong room. We're right next door, you know, and I never had a terribly good sense of direction. Believe me, both Captain Fraser and I were terribly embarrassed, and I think the sooner we let the poor man put some clothes on, the happier everyone will be." Except me, she thought belatedly, still hopelessly fascinated with his beautiful chest.

"Don't *you* be absurd, Elizabeth," Rupert snarled. "This man has been taking advantage of you, and I mean to see—"

"Rupert!" she shrieked, as Michael took a threatening step toward him.

"I would suggest, St. Ives, that you take that insult back," he said, his voice a silken menace. "Miss Traherne is hardly likely to submit to being ravished without putting up a fight, and she is, as you can see, looking charmingly intact."

"I'm ashamed of you, Rupert, for suspecting such a thing," she said in a high, breathless voice. "And I am certain Jeremy would be too. Now you come along with me to chapel while I read you a thundering scold for having such a wretched mind." She tugged at his sturdy figure, and after one last, bitter glance at Fraser's saturnine face, he followed her. When they were out of earshot, she could feel the tensed muscles relax.

"You don't fool me for a moment, Elizabeth," he said with grim amusement.

"Whatever do you mean? If you're going to suggest that I actually did anything with that insufferable, rude—"

"I know you didn't. And I beg pardon for thinking such a thing, even for a moment. The trouble is, I know what sort Fraser is."

"You also know what sort I am," she said stiffly.

"I do indeed. And I know you aren't the addle-brained widgeon you just did a very creditable imitation of. So I can only presume you are trying to protect Fraser. And I wonder why."

"I am not trying to protect him. But I also don't want you skewering him for something he didn't do," she shot back.

"He's earned it many times over for other crimes. Not the least of which is his current traitorous activities."

"What makes you think he's a traitor?" she demanded. "He's been a loyal soldier for years. Why should he turn bad?"

Rupert shrugged his massive shoulders. "It's the same old story. He was passed over for a promotion, a promotion I won't deny he more than deserved. That made him bitter, and his gaming debts made him vulnerable to offers of French assistance."

"Do you have any proof of this?" she asked hotly.

"We're getting it. In the meantime, you keep out of his rooms and out of his way. He'll be a dangerous man when cornered, you mark my word. Jeremy would never forgive me if anything happened to you."

"Nothing's going to happen to me. Not at Captain Fraser's hands, at any rate," she said with great certainty as they reached the chapel door. Rupert looked down at her, a troubled expression on his grim face, but he said nothing as he led her inside.

ELIZABETH HAD SAT through more painful services, but not many. Usually she was responsible for a goodly part of the sermon each week delivered in Sumner's thundering tones. But her brother, disdaining her advice, had chosen for his text "Esau, my brother, is a hairy man, and I am a smooth man." As Elizabeth sat demurely in the front pew of the small family chapel, she was fully aware of Adolphus's fulminating gaze, Lady Elfreda's unruffled good cheer, and the various bored expressions on those around her as they listened to her brother drone on and on. Every now and then Rupert would gaze down at her perplexedly, and she reached out and patted his strong hand reassuringly. As if he were another brother, she realized with a start of surprise.

Neither Brenna nor the contessa was anywhere in sight, and Elizabeth only hoped they hadn't murdered each other in a jealous rage over her brother. But considering the contessa's eventual destination last night, it seemed likely she wouldn't care. Fraser had likewise decided to avoid holy worship that morning, unless Adolphus had already speared him with a sword to avenge her tarnished honor. Surprisingly enough, she giggled again, incurring Sumner's disapproving glare.

Elizabeth had a strong sense of self-preservation, and she knew full well that the only thing that would stop the various people eager to upbraid her would be Sir Maurice. He was viewed by all present as something akin to the Prince Regent himself, albeit a trifle more distinguished. Adolphus bowed to his every pronouncement with flattering raptness, Fraser was politely deferential, Sir Henry Hatchett and Rupert were respectful, and Lady Elfreda viewed him with an awe that seemed almost to border on fear. After last night Elizabeth hesitated to place herself in reach of those hard, encroaching fingers and that mountainous stomach, but there was no help for it. Without a doubt no one would dare accost her for her behavior in the presence of the redoubtable general.

Therefore, once the interminable service was over, she darted up to Sir Maurice and with amazing temerity wove her arm through his, smiling at him confidingly.

"I haven't had any chance to talk with you again," she said with a coy simper. "I am so honored to be present at a houseparty with one of our most distinguished heroes. You must tell me all about your favorite battles."

The lecherous look he cast her would have panicked a less determined creature than Elizabeth. "You're the filly young Fraser has his eye on, eh? What game is it you're playing, m'dear?"

This was unpromising, but the look on Adolphus's moon face was decidedly dangerous, and Elizabeth persevered. "I expect we seem like silly, brainless creatures to a great soldier such as yourself," she continued valiantly, determined not to let him abandon her to the wolves. "But truly, I am fascinated by warfare and espionage and the like. I expect you've known a great many French agents."

He turned to stare at her slowly out of his dark, cruel eyes, and Elizabeth was vaguely aware that she had put her foot in it this time.

"Young lady, you shouldn't be worrying your pretty little head about such stuff. That's men's business, not for the weaker sex," he admonished sharply, and removed her hand from his arm with finality before turning his short, sturdy back on her. Elizabeth couldn't control a little shiver of relief. There was something about the man that unnerved her.

"Don't mind him." The contessa materialized by her side, looking surprisingly well rested considering her nighttime perambulations. "He doesn't care for intelligent females, I'm afraid."

"With you being the exception?" Elizabeth found herself saying, and then blushed. When would she learn to control her unruly tongue? "I beg your pardon. I had no right to say such a thing."

"That's perfectly all right. I take it as a compliment," the contessa said, her good humor unimpaired. "It's quite true that the general and I are more than friends, so why should I mind a little plain speaking? As a matter of fact, I prefer it. Why are Sir Adolphus and the old dragon staring at you so furiously? And the handsome Captain St. Ives is deep in conversation with your so-charming brother. The looks they keep casting your way are not encouraging."

"They caught me in Michael's room this morning," she confessed with a trace of defiance.

A delicately shaped eyebrow rose. "Did they, indeed? This sounds most promising. I suggest we go for a drive and escape from their overwatchful eyes. Then you can tell me all about it."

Elizabeth looked at her flawless beauty, the warm, friendly smile, and remembered Wat Simpkin and the midnight strolls. "I would love it. It won't take me a minute to get my pelisse."

"I'll come with you," the contessa offered. "That way no one can give you the bear jawing they're obviously longing for."

She smiled up at Elizabeth's superior height. "And we can pour out our girlish hearts and give each other much good advice, I don't doubt."

"I'll do my best," Elizabeth said, determined to learn more than she would offer.

It was obvious the contessa had the same object in mind. "I am certain you will," she replied in dulcet tones.

Chapter 15

IT HAD TURNED into quite a lovely day. As Elizabeth, attired in a walking dress of green merino that set off her sherry-colored eyes and chestnut hair to perfection, seated herself next to the contessa, she had to stifle a slight twinge of disappointment that Michael Fraser was nowhere about to admire her toilette.

It was through a kind fate that they had managed to avoid Sumner's condemning figure bearing down on them as they left the house, and his large blue eyes had a petulant expression in them as he turned and murmured something in an aggrieved tone to Rupert St. Ives, who scarcely looked more conciliatory. Rupert shook his head, placing a restraining hand on Sumner's well-muscled arm, and responded to Elizabeth's saucy little wave with a curt nod that nevertheless revealed a great deal of admiration in his cool, hazel eyes. But it was too late, my dear Rupert, she thought sadly as she climbed into the landau. At the age of seventeen there would have been nothing she would have liked better than to have excited such admiration from her brother's mature and glamorous friend. But now he merely seemed like a somewhat staid older brother. Her romantic fantasy was wrapped up elsewhere.

It was a beautiful spring day. Small puffs of white clouds were off in the horizon, the green grass had a delicious damp smell, promising new growth, and daffodils were out in the park. It made midnight excursions and French spies and ghastly executions seem a figment of a fevered imagination, far more fanciful than any French novel Elizabeth had ever read. But the mature and possibly dangerous woman beside her was real, and so was the danger to her brother Jeremy and others.

Elizabeth had little doubt the contessa was offering to divert her in order to give her confederate, whoever he really was, time to search the castle for that incriminating list of spies. But Sir Henry was alive on all counts, Rupert was even more suspicious than she was, and a famous soldier such as Sir Maurice with cold, cynical eyes wouldn't let anything past him. She leaned back against the squabs and viewed the bright day gloomily.

"You look rather down in the dumps," the contessa observed, handling the reins with a deft expertise that Elizabeth admired. "Has young Fraser been difficult?"

Elizabeth jumped, startled, and gave the contessa a brilliantly false smile. "Why should Captain Fraser have any effect on my state of mind?" she questioned brightly. "I was merely worried about Brenna and my brother," she added pointedly.

The contessa smiled with unimpaired good humor. "You needn't worry. Sumner saw me disappear with Adolphus last night and has decided I'm beyond saving. I'm sure, if you just leave well enough alone, your brother and Miss O'Shea will arrive at a mutually satisfactory understanding before the weekend is out. Sumner has had his fling and will be the better husband for it."

"It must be convenient for your conscience to believe that," Elizabeth said with some asperity, remembering Brenna's miserable green eyes.

"I have no conscience, Miss Traherne." She laughed. "I've knocked about this world for far too long and been in far too many tight places to allow myself the luxury of one. But then, I doubt I ever had one in the first place. One doesn't when one is brought up in Billingsgate."

"Billingsgate?" Elizabeth echoed, thinking she must have misunderstood.

"You wouldn't know it to listen to me now, would you? I was born Lonnie Castle to a Billingsgate fishwife and some sailor she couldn't even remember. I learned to fend for myself early on, aided and abetted by certain generous gentlemen who helped me with my accent and manners. By the time I was twenty, I was no longer Lonnie Castle of London but the Contessa Leonora di Castello, and I haven't looked back once."

Elizabeth was silenced for only a moment. "Why are you telling me this?" she demanded suspiciously.

"I thought we should be honest with each other. Too much is riding on the outcome of this weekend's work. The future of this country, a country I'm surprisingly fond of, and my own personal future. I want to live a more settled existence, and I've decided Sir Adolphus will suit me just fine."

"Does he agree?" she questioned curiously.

"Oh, I have little doubt that he will. I have a way with men," the contessa murmured with a humble smile.

"I wish you all the luck in the world," said Elizabeth. "What can I do to further your success?"

"Don't care for him much yourself, do you? That's all right. He's a generous sort, full of juice, and that's the sort of gentleman I find most appealing. Not that I don't admire broad shoulders and a rakish air, but I learned long ago that Michael Fraser isn't for the likes of me."

Elizabeth's profound depression settled back over her. "Nor for me, either."

"I wouldn't be so sure of that. He's paid you far more attention than I've ever seen him waste on a young lady in the seven years I've known him Of course, he was married to that tiresome Marianne for part of that time, but the fever carried her off quite fortuitously."

"Fever?" Elizabeth echoed. "I thought it was childbirth."

"Not with Marianne She made certain her life wouldn't be cluttered up with the little creatures. I have little doubt the fever that carried her off was brought on by getting rid of one. Not that I disapprove of such drastic measures in certain circumstances, but she carried it too far. She really was the most wretched creature. Always whining and complaining when Michael was around and then casting those sly blue eyes at anything in pants when his back was turned. He should have known better than to have married to please his family. Even they agreed it was a miserable mistake."

"Blue eyes?" Elizabeth echoed, remembering Lady Elfreda's words.

"Blond-haired, blue-eyed, no bigger than a minute. One of those fragile, clinging types, always weeping and complaining."

"But Lady Elfreda said she looked exactly like me!"

"Haven't you learned by now that you cannot trust a word that old harridan has to say? I can't imagine two creatures more dissimilar than you and Marianne. You can be sure that Michael knows the difference." She cast a questioning look out of her saucy eyes. "But what I'm more interested in right now, my dear Elizabeth, is what Wat Simpkin had to say to you when you pretended to be me yesterday morning."

Elizabeth hesitated but then decided that frankness might avail her of more information. "I didn't pretend to be you. He merely jumped to that conclusion."

"A matter of semantics," she replied, dismissing Elizabeth's words airily. "What exactly did he tell you?"

"Why don't you ask him?" Elizabeth countered.

"Because he's disappeared. I suppose he realized his mistake and didn't care to be around for the consequences. Or perhaps our mutual friend Fredericks got rid of him. Or he might have decided, quite rightly, that his services are no longer required. Whatever, he's gone, and it's up to you to tell me how indiscreet he's been."

Elizabeth wavered for only a moment. The contessa had been more than frank so far, and her only hope of learning more seemed to demand an equal frankness. "He told me that a French agent named LeBoeuf had hidden a list of English agents active in France right now somewhere at Winfields and that one of the guests there is a French agent determined to retrieve that information, no matter what the cost. He didn't tell me who, but he did say that the government suspected the culprit. And I gather you might want to find the paper first and sell it to the government. Or to Napoleon?"

"Never. Wat Simpkin didn't know my reputation very well if he thought I'd get involved in that sort of stuff. I'm out for myself first of all, but elastic as my sense of morality is, it doesn't include selling out my country. Did he tell you where the paper was hidden?"

"He didn't seem to know. Do you?"

"Haven't the foggiest. At this point I presume only our friend the spy knows."

"Do you mean Michael Fraser?" Elizabeth's voice was surprisingly strong as she asked the question she dreaded to hear answered.

A small smile curved the contessa's ripe red lips. "You'd like me to tell you, wouldn't you? And do you know what would happen if you were to find out that the spy is Michael Fraser or some other member of this jolly little houseparty? You would probably not survive another hour. The person we're dealing with is cunning, desperate, and quite, quite ruthless. It would mean nothing to him to kill you."

"Is it Michael?" Her voice cracked in desperation.

"I'm not going to tell you," the contessa replied simply. "What you should do, my girl, is return to Winfields and glue yourself to Lady Elfreda. Sit there and tat, or read sermons, or play silver loo, or stare out the window. And ignore everything that seems the slightest bit untoward. You've been far too rambunctious so far, and I can't answer for the consequences if you don't do as I tell you."

"I have no intentions of doing anything unless you are honest with me."

"Wretched girl!" The contessa shook her head ruefully. "It's no wonder Michael's half out of his mind with frustration. I wonder your brothers haven't strangled you long ago."

"They're too afraid of me," she shot back. She eyed the contessa speculatively, hesitating for a moment. "I wonder if I could ask you a question?"

"Not if you're going to ask me who the spy is."

"Nothing to do with that. Or not much. I wondered . . . in light of your varied experiences . . . you must have seen a great many gentlemen without their shirts on."

The contessa smiled with reminiscent fondness. "That I have, dearie."

"And I don't doubt you've seen Captain Fraser without his shirt," she continued, stifling the pang that assailed her at such a thought.

The contessa nodded. "Not that it's ever done me much good. He's the one that got away, I'm afraid. A bit too fastidious to be interested in the likes of me. Ah, well, it's his loss."

"Is . . . that is, do most gentlemen look like Captain Fraser without their shirts? In the general run of things?"

"In the general run of things Michael Fraser has one of the most delightful bodies I've ever seen on a man. And I've seen quite a few," she added with a smile that could almost, on a gentleman, be called a leer. "Fancy him, do you?"

"Heavens, no!"

"Heavens, no!" she mimicked. "I've got eyes in my head, missy. Do as I tell you, and everything might just possibly come round right. Keep interfering, and heaven knows what will happen!" She cast a sharp look at her companion and let out a small sigh of exasperation. "You are the most frustrating girl!"

LUNCHEON WAS A prolonged, exceedingly boring affair, the entire proceedings enlivened only by the fulminating glances Brenna kept casting at the cow-eyed and repentant Sumner. Apparently the contessa was right, and he had seen the error of his ways. Elizabeth could only hope it wasn't too late. Brenna O'Shea was possessed of a good Irish temper, and the recent blow on her head hadn't helped it any.

On Elizabeth's left sat a preoccupied Rupert St. Ives, who spent fully as much time glaring across at Michael Fraser as Brenna did staring at Sumner. On Elizabeth's other side sat the taciturn General Wingert, who had obviously decided she was a flighty female who didn't know her place. To her wittiest overtures the dour Sir Maurice returned only monosyllabic answers, reserving the majority of his attention for his subdued adjutant.

Michael studiously avoided her questioning eyes during the meal, a grim expression around his mouth, a hint of anger in the dark blue eyes. The contessa spent her time flirting with a vastly pleased Adolphus, and Lady Elfreda, left with only Sir Henry to fall back on, decided to flirt archly with him. Poor Sir Henry appeared acutely uncomfortable, and every now and then he cast beseeching eyes toward Rupert. But the latter was too busy fuming at Fraser to notice.

Even the French chef's best efforts failed to rouse Elizabeth's appetite. When the moment came for the ladies to withdraw, she hastily excused herself, pleading a dire headache.

She was halfway up the stairs to her bedroom when Sumner's rich, golden voice reached her. "Elizabeth!" he thundered in his best Revelation's voice. "Come back down here immediately!"

She halted, one slender foot on the step above her, and contemplated whether she dared pretend not to have heard him. But she had hesitated too long, and she might as well face Sumner's righteous indignation now rather than later. If he was unable to vent his spleen, his rage would only build.

"I have a headache," she offered plaintively.

"Caused by guilt, I have no doubt," he replied in a repressive voice, squaring his manly shoulders. "Will you come down or shall I have to come up and drag you down?"

Sumner had always been somewhat of a bully despite his gentle appearance, and Jeremy was no longer around to protect her. "Very well," she sighed with a martyred air as she descended the staircase. Like a recalcitrant child she found herself led into the deserted ballroom, the door shut firmly behind her fuming brother. The room was a great deal larger and less welcoming in the cold bright light of day, and Elizabeth availed herself of one of the delicate gilt chairs with a weary sigh.

"I would prefer you to stand," Sumner scowled.

"Oh, cut line, brother," she snapped back, not in the proper mood for this. "Let's have it and be done with it. I have far too much on my mind to have to deal with your jawing at me."

Sumner's handsome face took on a deeply sorrowful expression. "Elizabeth, this willful attitude of yours grieves me deeply. I couldn't believe my ears when Rupert told me what you were doing this morning! Are you lost to every vestige of propriety? To be found alone in a man's bedroom, with the gentleman in question undressed—"

"He was wearing a towel!" Elizabeth interrupted.

"Oh, marvelous," Sumner said, his voice heavy with sarcasm. "And that makes everything right and proper, I suppose. If it were anyone else, I would insist that the man marry you and save your reputation, but in the case of a confirmed villain such as Michael Fraser we may only hope that no word of this gets out. I am certain I can trust the Wingerts and the contessa to keep silent, and Rupert would lay down his life to protect your reputation. But Fraser is another matter. I am afraid he might try to blackmail us, and there will be nothing we can do but pay him. That a sister of mine, a vicar's sister, should embroil herself in such a hideous tangle horrifies and grieves me. What Jeremy would say if he were to hear of this contretemps I shudder to think."

"Are you quite finished?" Elizabeth inquired in deceptively affable tones.

"Hardly. Do you realize what a dangerous fellow Fraser is? Rupert has been telling me the most horrifying tales. Sir Henry Hatchett came here accompanied by half a dozen soldiers. Their purpose I don't dare to guess, but you may be sure it involves Michael Fraser! Cousin Adolphus and I have discussed the matter, of course, and had hoped we had guaranteed the safety of our womenfolk, but I have found our confidence to be sadly misplaced. I should have known *you* would involve yourself needlessly. It has long been a sorrow to me that you refuse to be guided by my wise counsel, ignore my advice, and go running off without—"

"Sumner!" Elizabeth's voice could thunder on occasion, and it did just then. Her brother subsided into a surprised mumble. She rose to her full height and stared up at him defiantly, her golden eyes furious. "What I do, and with whom I do it, is none of your business."

"Don't be absurd!" he protested ineffectually, still rather awed by her volume. "I'm your brother, the head of the household in Jeremy's absence; of course you should defer to me."

"You, my dear Sumner, are a cod's head," she said in scathing tones. "You've been so busy running after a pretty lightskirt who's scarcely your sort of female that you've thrown away a fine girl who loves you desperately. And for what? Brenna's sick of you, and well she ought to be. The contessa has far bigger fish than you in mind, and you dare to criticize my behavior. I wonder you have the nerve."

Sumner opened his mouth, shut it, and then opened it again as he gathered force. "Are you trying to defend your behavior with Captain Fraser by attacking mine?" he demanded in awesome tones.

"I am neither defending it nor apologizing for it. It's none of your business."

Sumner's strong, handsome jaw snapped shut, and the baby blue eyes blazed furiously. "Are you intending to carry on with your disgusting behavior with that . . . that traitor, as Rupert informs me?"

"Rupert has been a bit too busy informing people," she shot back. "I'll do what I damn well please."

"And did you learn cursing from your handsome spy?" he questioned hotly.

She allowed a saucy smile to wreathe her face. "Among other things."

The slight hold Sumner had on his temper vanished. "How dare you!" he thundered, his voice carrying, probably into every room, Elizabeth thought distractedly. "If you insist on continuing this . . . this disgusting behavior, then you will leave me no choice in the matter." He started toward the door, then stopped and turned to deliver the crushing blow. "Elizabeth," he said in ringing tones, "you are no sister of mine."

"Almost, brother dear, you persuade me," she replied silkily, and then winced as the door slammed shut behind him.

She sat back down on the gilt chair for a moment, surprised to discover that she was trembling. Hot as her temper could be, she still disliked quarreling with her overbearing brother above all things. Shouting voices made her physically ill, and she leaned back against the chair and shut her eyes for a moment

The sound of a distinctly feminine gasp came to Elizabeth's tired ears.

"Brenna!" Sumner's usually rounded tones were somewhat ragged.

"Sumner Traherne," Brenna's furious voice carried in to Elizabeth's curious attention, "if you think you can treat me like this, you have another thing—" Her voice was cut off abruptly, and Elizabeth rose from her chair and moved closer to the door, unashamedly pressing one ear against the carved paneling. There was now no sound in the hallway except a curious rustling noise.

And then Sumner's voice, little more than a whisper, drifted in. "Forgive me, Brenna," he said simply. More rustlings followed, a deep sigh, and then Brenna's voice, strangely husky, said, "Oh. Sumner."

Elizabeth deemed it time to retire. Perhaps her brother had seen the error of his ways. Perhaps he wasn't such a gudgeon after all, but she'd place no reliance on it. With a sigh she moved back across the deserted ballroom to the French doors.

A furtive movement out in the depths of the garden seized her wandering attention. Without hesitation she silently turned the latch on the French doors and slipped out onto the terrace. The sunny morning had given way to a cloudy afternoon, and the shadowy garden seemed a gloomy place for a walk. Perhaps she had imagined that movement off in the distance. Then she saw them.

Three men were deep in conversation. Even from that distance Elizabeth could detect the general's squat, almost malevolent form, and there was no mistaking Sir Henry's gray mane of hair. But the tall, straight form of a younger man beside them as they moved slowly in her direction, lost in conversation, was not immediately recognizable. He wasn't tall enough or graceful enough to be Fraser. And it wasn't the hauntingly familiar-unfamiliar shape of the mysterious Fredericks from Starfield Cove. It could only be Rupert, though what they could be talking about excited Elizabeth's attention to no small degree. Very discreetly she slipped off the balcony and crept forward, hoping against hope that she might overhear something of interest.

It didn't take her long to come upon Michael Fraser, who obviously had the same intentions. His tall, straight back was to her as he hid behind an accommodating thicket, so intent on the conversation that he failed to hear her silent approach. Elizabeth stared at him meditatively for one long moment, the trace of a smile on her full lips. The captain was not quite as professional as he hoped to be. Unable to resist the temptation, she crept up behind him and tapped him lightly on the shoulder.

With a muffled curse he spun around, and there was a flash of steel from the wicked-looking knife in his hand. They stared at each other for a long moment.

"Were you planning to kill me with that?" she inquired politely. "Or had you reserved that honor for one of those three gentlemen?"

With a grim expression he tucked the knife back into his boot. "I wasn't planning to kill anyone, Lizzie," he replied in a whisper. "Though you may very well drive me to it. Go away."

"I will not. I want to hear what they have to say fully as much as you do," she whispered back pertly. "And if you don't let me, I will go and interrupt them, and then you will find out exactly nothing."

"I think I will murder you," he said in a savage undertone, yanking her into the bushes with him. "Keep your mouth quiet or it will be here and now."

She did as she was told, staring at the three approaching figures with silent determination. The only problem with her vantage point was its proximity to Michael Fraser. However much she might want to strain her ears for any stray words, watch closely for any revealing expression, all she could concentrate on was the tall, lean body directly behind her, so close she could feel the heat emanating from him, feel his breath stir her hair, hear the quiet sound of his breathing. More than anything she longed to lean back against that strong, comforting body and be enfolded in those arms.

Pay attention, she ordered herself savagely. Listen to what they're saying. Remember Jeremy and what you owe him. Don't forget the danger, Brenna's knock on the head, the poor drowned Frenchman, the mysteriously familiar figure down at Starfield Cove. Most of all, don't forget Jeremy.

A small gasp escaped her as she turned accusingly to Fraser, her brown eyes wide with shock. "It was Jeremy!" she cried in a mercifully quiet shriek. "How could I be so stupid? It was Jeremy down at the cove. It was Jeremy."

With more force than was strictly necessary Michael clapped a hand over her mouth and dragged her down into the bushes. "For God's sake, be quiet," he breathed in her ear. "If you want to save your brother's life, keep that damned mouth shut."

The voices were ominously close. "What was that?" The high-pitched, authoritarian tones could only belong to General Wingert. "I heard voices, Hatchett."

"Did you, Maurice?" that gentleman returned affably. "I can't say I did, but then, my hearing is not what it was. Did you hear anything, St. Ives?"

"Damn it, I'm not asking for opinions!" the general snapped. "Search those bushes, St. Ives. If someone is spying on us, I want to know who."

"Yes, sir." Rupert's voice was even closer. Out of panicked eyes Elizabeth could see his sturdy legs as he thrashed about the bushes directly in front of them. Fraser's hand was still clapped across her mouth, his grip numbing her arm as he held her in a crouch under the shield of the boxwood.

"Check behind you, man!" the general snapped, and Elizabeth's heart sank.

"Very good, sir." Rupert came directly toward them, parted the bushes and looked down into Elizabeth's frightened eyes and the hand across her mouth. There was absolutely no change in his expression.

He let the bushes go back over them. "No one here, sir," he said blandly. "It must have been the ravens."

"I grew up here, Captain. We've never had ravens before," Sir Maurice said testily, and their voices trailed away. "So you'll be leaving me to keep an eye on the place this evening, eh, Hatchett? While you go off on some wild goose chase."

"We think we've found something interesting, Maurice," Sir Henry replied genially. "Down at the cove, where LeBoeuf was found. I doubt anything will happen during the short time we're gone. If you'd like, we can leave a couple of my men behind."

"No need for that," the general replied, suddenly affable. "I think an old war-horse like me can be trusted to see to the safety of a bunch of females. The day I can't . . ."

The voices faded beyond hearing, and Fraser slowly loosened his strangling grip, stretching to his full height and pulling Elizabeth up beside him. There was no sign of the three gentlemen.

"What is going on here?" Elizabeth exploded once she had caught her breath. "What in the world are you up to? Is Rupert a traitor, too? And my brother?" Her voice was high-pitched with anxiety.

"There is no need to get hysterical," Fraser said in a repressive voice. "And you might as well resign yourself to the fact that I am going to tell you exactly nothing. I would strongly suggest you go inside and spend your time pursuing some improving activity. And keep out of the way. If you're a good girl, I'll explain it all to you tomorrow." He gave her a little push.

"If I'm a good girl?" she echoed, infuriated. "I'm going to stop you, Michael Fraser. I'm not going to let you get away with whatever it is you're doing, and I'm not going to let you drag Rupert and Jeremy down with you."

"And what," he inquired casually, "has convinced you that I am such a villain? Has it ever occurred to you for one moment that I might be on the side of the angels?"

"No," she snapped. "I know you far too well."

"After two days? I take leave to doubt that. However, my sweet termagant, you'll have a chance to remedy that before long. In the meantime, go back inside. I have some thinking to do."

"With pleasure," she said icily, flouncing away. Keep out of the way, she fumed. *Oh, you'd like that very well, my fine Captain Fraser. But I am going to do no such thing. I am going to find General Wingert and tell him exactly what is going on. And then we'll see who's so clever.*

But then I might be betraying Jeremy, she thought belatedly as she let herself into the deserted ballroom from the terrace. *I don't dare do that, and well Michael knows that. He knows that I daren't trust anyone, that I have no choice but to do just as he tells me. The only person I can turn to is myself.* The thought was scarcely reassuring.

Stepping out into the hallway, she started for the stairs. The general and his compatriots would be deep in their schemes for some time yet. Most of the ladies, with the possible exception of the Contessa of Billingsgate, would be much too involved in their own business to come in search of her. But the contessa had drunk a formidable amount of wine with lunch, and there was little doubt she was at that moment reposing sleepily by the fire, her heavy lids drooping over her usually sharp eyes. Michael would be too caught up in his chicanery to keep an eye on her while she snooped.

Please let it be all right, she prayed silently as she crept along the deserted corridor. Jeremy couldn't be a traitor! *Sweet heaven, don't let Rupert be betraying his country and leading his oldest and dearest friend astray. Let him be on Jeremy's side. And oh, dear God, let Michael Fraser be on his side, too.* Or I shall kill him with my own bare hands, she promised grimly.

As Elizabeth had suspected, there was a large mahogany desk in the center of the small sitting room that opened onto Sir Maurice's bedroom. The top was littered with papers and broken pens and several books open at various strategic passages. The curtains were drawn against the cloudy day, and she didn't dare pull them back to allow any more light into the room. She leaned over the desk, peering at the papers, her face screwed up into a frown as she tried to make sense of the various dispatches, notes, reports, and the like, hoping against hope that she'd find the answers to the thousand questions that were racketing around in her brain. It was beyond her. There was nothing that could help her decide just how villainous the men she loved most were.

So engrossed was she in trying to decipher the contents of one particular missive that she failed to hear the door open, failed to notice the large, menacing figure that crept up silently behind her. She heard the faint creaking, and then a heavy object crashed down on her head, and she collapsed with a small sigh into a graceless heap on the red Turkey carpet, leaving her assailant staring down at her with mixed emotions.

Chapter 16

IT WAS DARK AND cold, and Elizabeth was extremely uncomfortable. For one thing, her wrists and ankles were tied together with ruthless bonds that felt as if they were made of ground glass but doubtless were in actuality rough hemp. They had seen fit to tie her onto a chair, placing a gag in her mouth so that she couldn't scream for help once she regained consciousness. She tried to wriggle but found herself unable to move. As the pain in her head suddenly made itself known, she decided quickly that she preferred not to move or even breathe as long as that shattering pain continued.

Her memory, along with her thinking processes, was a trifle hazy. It was with great effort that she remembered standing over Sir Maurice's desk. And then, nothing. Not even a flash of blinding pain, though her head was now busily making up for its original forbearance. She could see nothing and wondered if they had put a blindfold over her eyes. She squinted but could feel no cloth across her face. Indeed, as she became accustomed to the dark, a faint glimmer of light appeared in the direction of where her feet should be. Moving her aching head backward, she felt rough wool suspended over her head, and against her cheek the faint coolness of a metal button. Someone's closet, then. The question was, whose?

But more important, thought Elizabeth, shedding easy tears of pain and exhaustion, was ridding herself of this demonic headache. With a snuffle and a small sigh, she shut her eyes again and fell asleep.

The voices woke her. By this time the thin ribbon of light beneath the closet door was fainter, and she vaguely wondered what time it could possibly be. Surely someone would miss her before long and come searching for her? She could only hope she had been placed in the closet of an occupied room, though the coats hanging above her seemed to suggest she need have no fears on that score. If someone had trundled her off into one of the uninhabited bedrooms, she might not be found until. . . . The thought was quite horrid, and Elizabeth began struggling at her bonds with renewed vigor. She wasn't about to submit tamely to being bludgeoned and trussed up like a capon, she thought furiously, ignoring the pounding of her poor abused skull. As soon as she found out who dared to assault her, she would. . . .

Suitable revenges danced pleasurably in her mind as she applied herself to her bonds, which were proving not quite as incapacitating as previously.

The voices came again, and Elizabeth halted her struggles. The first voice was unfamiliar to her ears. The second one she recognized with a cheerful gnashing of teeth and renewed fervor toward her bonds.

"May I help you, sir?" It was an upper-class servant's accent.

Fraser's voice came back in clipped businesslike tones. "I don't think so, Holmes. I was merely checking to see if I left a dispatch on the general's desk. I don't seem to find it, however."

"I'll tell him you were looking, sir."

The voice was sepulchral and ever so faintly threatening. Elizabeth leaned back, digesting the information as she listened to the two pairs of footsteps move away, the door open and close, and then the silence closing in once more. So she was in General Wingert's bedroom, just off the sitting room. Her assailant hadn't been able to carry her farther than the nearest closet. Perhaps there were advantages to being taller and more generously endowed than most women.

A moment later the door opened again, quietly, surreptitiously, and a single set of footsteps entered the room. There was the quiet sound of opening and closing drawers, the rustle of papers, the creak of the bed, and then loud voices from out in the hall. The footsteps in the room moved quickly, directly toward the closet.

The dusky light of evening blinded her as the door was flung open, and then a figure blocked it out, tripping over her in his haste to conceal himself and in the process giving her a nasty thwack on the shin. The door shut behind him, and she was trapped in the closet with a nefarious stranger.

She was in no way surprised when Fraser's explosive whisper came to her ear. "So there's where you got to," he said coldheartedly. "Who had the good sense to tie you up and toss you in here?"

Her response was a muffled "*mmphhh*" before his hand reached over her gag and silenced her. "Be quiet," he whispered, "or you may not live to make another sound if those two should hear us."

It was the same servant's voice from before. "I have no idea what Captain Fraser was doing in the room, sir. You told me he'd have no reason to go through the contents of your desk without you present, and yet not five minutes ago I found him, cool as you please, sorting through that pile of papers there."

"I don't know if I quite trust the good captain, Holmes," General Wingert's high-pitched voice came back to the two eavesdroppers "He came highly recommended, but I somehow doubt his loyalty to me. He's the only one who knows enough to cause any difficulty tonight. Since he hasn't accompanied Sir Henry on his little ride, we may have to do something about him. If not this evening, then in the next few days. A riding accident, perhaps?" There was a meditative tone to his girlish voice.

"Would you like me to see to it, sir?" Holmes inquired in the tone of voice one would use to inquire whether the stockings were suitable for evening wear.

"Perhaps. We shall see how this night's work goes. He may have a chance to demonstrate his loyalty to me. Which direction did he go in?"

"I believe back downstairs. That nosy Traherne girl has disappeared. No doubt he'll be trying to find her."

"Excellent! Leonora and Adolphus are busy in a mad flirtation, and m'sister-in-law is sound asleep by the fire. I gather that bone-headed vicar is off trying to make up with the Irish chit, and Hatchett and the others have headed off by now. We should have only Fraser to worry about. And since he's clearly besotted with the Traherne wench, he should be no problem at all. If he is, I'm sure I can count on you to back me up if I need assistance."

"Certainly, General Wingert. Were you planning to retrieve the list now?"

Elizabeth drew an involuntary gasp of breath, and she felt Fraser's hot breath on her cheek. "Don't make a sound, Lizzie," he breathed, his lips brushing her skin. She squirmed in protest, moving closer to him. He seemed to take that as a sign of encouragement and continued to move his mouth along her cheek, down her neck, leaving a trail of burning kisses that completely distracted her. All the while he was listening intently to the general's treasonous plans.

"There could hardly be a better time. We're due to leave tomorrow morning, and I don't fancy wandering around the battlements at two o'clock in the morning. Besides, Leonora might choose this night of all nights to spend the entire time in my bed, and then what would I do? I don't trust the trollop further than I could throw her. She and Adolphus will make an excellent pair. The fat fool." The first pair of footsteps moved across the room. "Where's the coat, Holmes? I want the pouch in the lining. You'll take it to France yourself this time. LeBoeuf couldn't have chosen a worse time to get himself killed. We'll have to be doubly careful this time."

"The gray coat, sir?" he inquired anxiously, and with mounting horror Elizabeth heard his shuffling gait moving directly toward the closet. Fraser gave her a tiny little bite on the collarbone before continuing with his demoralizing little kisses. He began to undo the buttons at the back of her neck.

"Not in there, fool! Do you think I'd leave it in the closet for anyone to find? I told you I didn't trust Fraser. It's in the bottom drawer of the blanket press. That's the ticket." The tone of satisfaction was evident, and Elizabeth breathed a little sigh of relief. Fraser's mouth moved across her throat.

"That's it, then." There was a curious note in the old man's voice, both of exultation and of nervousness. Like a bride on her wedding night, Elizabeth thought as Fraser's mouth edged lower.

She made a small protesting noise as she moved closer to his commanding body, her movements hampered by the chair attached to her trim ankles. A small, silent laugh shook Fraser, and deft fingers reached up and slipped the gag from her mouth. She had scarcely a moment to draw a breath before his hot, hungry mouth covered hers. And then everything faded from consideration: the list, Jeremy, the traitorous general. There was no reality but the velvet darkness and his mouth on hers as time and space ceased to exist.

The door closed into the hallway with a decisive snap, and the sound of the general's brisk gait faded in the distance. Before Elizabeth could begin to divine Fraser's intention, that questing mouth left hers, the door was flung open, and the tall, cadaverous figure of Holmes, the general's valet, was lying on the floor, knocked unconscious by Fraser's speedy deftness and a handy Sevres vase. He turned back to Elizabeth, his expression unreadable in the dimly lit room.

"Sorry, darling. I think I'll leave you there where you won't cause any more trouble," he said lightly. Before she could open her mouth to protest, he had slipped the gag back over her. "There," he said, a note of satisfaction in his voice. "That should keep you until I return." She cast him a mute, furious glance out of her sherry-colored eyes. He moved back to her side, kissed her on her freckled nose, and smiled down at her beguilingly.

"I do hope you pay more attention to my wishes when we're married, my love," he said sweetly, and there was a light of devil-may-care happiness in the dark blue eyes. He's enjoying this, she thought furiously. *Thriving on the danger, and I'm terrified.* "You stay right there while I get help, Lizzie, and someone will be back in no time at all."

She let out a muffled squeak of fury, but he merely patted her on the top of her tousled head and ran from the room.

Elizabeth's rage gave her new strength. The knots had already been loosened from her steady struggles, and with renewed determination she wrestled with them, ignoring the pain in her wrists. Her assailant, whoever he might have been, certainly lacked experience, because within five minutes she was able to free her hands, and she was flying down the hall without even a passing glance for the recumbent Holmes. Only one of the battlements was accessible, the east one, and she had no doubt that General Wingert was now well on his way, secure in the knowledge that no one could catch him. Not a sensitive man, the general. He hadn't felt the net closing in around him. Well, she would do her part to prove him wrong. While Fraser went romping around looking for reinforcements, she would witness his foul treason and be ready to testify to it.

She could hear Wingert up ahead of her on the winding steps. Despite his lengthy head start he fortunately had been in no hurry, convinced that all interested parties were safely accounted for. Not that he'd think a mere female to be of any moment. She could see him dimly up ahead, his short, squat form illuminated by the lamp he was carrying, shedding just enough light for Elizabeth to see her way up the winding turret behind him. Her Morocco slippers had heavy soles, and she gave a precious minute to taking them off, leaving them neatly in a corner as she continued on in stocking feet, noiselessly, her attention on the evil figure up ahead as it neared the parapet door.

The lamp up ahead flickered in the wind, and then Elizabeth was plunged into total darkness as the general vanished onto the parapet. Abandoning all thought of caution, she flew up the stairs behind him, her mind dwelling fretfully on bats. The stairs came to an abrupt halt, and she banged into a solid object that could only be the door, winding herself. Before she could hide, that door was flung open, and Sir Maurice Wingert stood there in all his fury, staring up at her tall, disheveled figure with acute loathing.

"I should have known it would be you," he said fiercely, grabbing her arm in a surprisingly strong grip and dragging her out onto the windblown parapet. The moon was silvery bright overhead, now and then obscured by scudding clouds, and the tower glistened in the eerie light. They were alone out there, the two of them in the windswept night air, and Elizabeth knew she could expect no mercy from the furious traitor in front of her. Despite his lack of height, he more than made up for it in strength and rage. Elizabeth knew she would stand no chance against him. "How did you know I would be here?" he demanded hoarsely. "Who else knows where I've gone?"

"I was tied up in your closet," she shot back, her voice coming in an irritatingly frightened croak. "And Captain Fraser was there with me. He's gone for help right now. You might as well give up, you know. You'll never get away with it."

"If you expect me to believe that wild tale, young lady," the general snarled, "then you're a greater fool than I took you for. You're helping Hatchett out, aren't you? You aren't that idiot parson's sister at all but an agent just like Leonora. That's it, isn't it? Well, you knew what risks you were taking. Move over to the edge."

"Michael!" she screamed desperately, hopelessly, as she read the murder in his eyes. "Help me." The wind took her cries and carried them out into the night. She knew it would be no use, and therefore it was with great disbelief that she saw him appear in the doorway, the wind whipping his dark hair, the moon shadowing the distant planes of his handsome face. He stood there for a moment, taking in the general's menacing form, Elizabeth cowering by the edge.

"What's going on, sir?" he questioned in a low, evil voice, and Elizabeth stared at him in gaping amazement.

"You know perfectly well what's going on, Fraser!" the general snapped. "Are you with me?"

"Of course, sir. You know I always have been."

"Then kill that stupid wench. Throttle her," the old man screamed in a frenzy. Without hesitation Michael started toward her.

"No, Michael," she whimpered as his beautiful hands reached around her throat, the throat that a few short minutes ago had burned with his kisses, and the broad thumbs began to press against her windpipe. "No," she begged, staring up at him with tear-filled eyes.

"Hurry up," the general ordered, fumbling with a section of the wall. Michael's hands tightened.

Chapter 17

THROUGH THE PANIC that filled her came an insistent whisper. "Swoon, damn you," Michael hissed between clenched teeth. In relief, Elizabeth let every muscle in her body go slack, tumbling to the stone floor in a graceless sprawl, hitting both knees, her cheek, and an elbow with agonizing force. She kept her eyes shut out of self-preservation, content to lie there unmoving with the wind whistling above her and the two desperate men beside her.

The grating of stone upon stone was unpleasantly close to her ear, and the cry of satisfaction from Sir Maurice's high-pitched voice was equally jarring. "Here's the damned thing. See to the girl, Fraser, and then we'll retire to my rooms to celebrate."

"I think not," Sir Henry Hatchett's cool voice broke through, and Elizabeth opened one eye in a tentative squint to see the surprisingly capable looking figure illuminated in the doorway, with a shadowy, achingly familiar form directly behind him. "I arrest you, Sir Maurice Wingert, on the charge of treason."

"Don't be absurd, Hatchett!" The general turned around slowly, an innocent expression on his face. "What maggot have you got in your brain? Treason? I never heard anything more absurd."

"And what is that you have in your hand, Sir Maurice?" Fraser inquired in silken tones. "*Billets-doux?*"

As Elizabeth pulled her aching body into a sitting position, a joyous cry broke from her lips. "Jeremy!"

Jeremy's dear, familiar face had an unaccustomedly grim expression as his eyes flickered toward his battered sister. "Be quiet, Elizabeth," he ordered sternly. "Sounds as if you've caused more than your share of trouble these last few days. It's a wonder Michael didn't really throttle you."

A snarl deformed the general's florid countenance. "I should have known, Fraser," he said mildly enough, holding his pudgy fist up into the wind, the papers clutched in pale white fingers. Before anyone could move, the fingers released their grip, and the papers sailed off into the wind, over the parapet and down toward the courtyard.

Fraser swore long and brilliantly before racing off the platform and down the stairs, with Jeremy directly behind him. Sir Henry had a very serviceable pistol trained on the center of the general's ample middle, and the milky blue eyes no longer looked quite so mild.

"Are you all right, Miss Traherne?" Sir Henry questioned, not taking his eyes off his quarry's truculent figure.

"A trifle bruised, but nothing to signify," she said, brushing the dirt off her pale green dress as she got to her feet.

"You won't be able to make any charges stick, you know," the general said in a conversational tone. "Those papers will never be seen again, and who would be likely to take Fraser's word against that of a Wingert?"

"There's also my word and that of my brother," Elizabeth said sturdily, glaring at him.

"A country nobody and a mere lieutenant," he said, dismissing them. "Admit it, Henry. You're beaten."

Indeed, Sir Henry was looking a trifle discomfited. "If anyone can find the evidence, Fraser can," he said simply. "He's one of my best men. What with Traherne and St. Ives down there helping, I'd back the three of them to find it."

"You haven't a chance," the general said amiably, leaning back against the parapet and looking perfectly at home. "How long do you intend to keep me here, Henry? It's a trifle chilly."

"Until Fraser sends a detail of my men up," he replied. "And I believe I hear them now."

Indeed, a great deal of noise was coming rapidly closer up the stairs. It was with surprise not unmixed with amusement that Elizabeth recognized Adolphus's portly, red-faced figure stagger onto the parapet, huffing and puffing more loudly than an entire regiment.

"That's the . . . most . . . ghastly . . . climb," he wheezed, his eyes watering. "Must have . . . something . . . done about . . . those . . . steps. Haven't been . . . up here . . . in . . . years." He blinked at the odd tableau, took two long, shuddering gasps, and forced himself to breathe with a semblance of normality. "I say, Sir Henry, what's going on here? Why have you got a gun pointed at m'uncle? And did I pass my cousin Jeremy on the way up here? I thought he was in France."

"Yes, that was Jeremy Traherne," Sir Henry explained patiently. "He's been in the country for several weeks now on a special assignment for me, an assignment that has concerned General Wingert. I am afraid your uncle stands accused of a very serious crime, Sir Adolphus. He's been caught red-handed in treasonous activities."

"My uncle?" he echoed fretfully, yet Elizabeth had the distinct impression that it came as no surprise at all to him. "This won't do at all, Sir Henry. If I had known it was my uncle you had your eye on, I would never have invited you to Winfields. Dash it, it's just not done. You don't accept a fellow's hospitality and then up and arrest his uncle. What will my mother say?" Apparently this last thought was the most devastating, for his red face turned purple in dismay.

"We'll do our utmost to spare Lady Elfreda any undue unpleasantness," Sir Henry said in a soothing voice.

"No way you can do that," Adolphus pointed out with great reasonableness. "Best thing is to let the old fellow go. I'm certain he'll promise never to do it again, won't you, Uncle?"

"Adolphus, sometimes your foolishness astounds even me," said the general in pained tones.

"I'm afraid that's out of the question, Sir Adolphus. The general will have to stand trial."

"And I will most certainly be acquitted."

"Possibly," Sir Henry allowed. "But not if I have anything to say about it."

Adolphus's florid moon face took on a contemplative

expression. "I wonder, Sir Henry, if I might be allowed a few words with my uncle in private? After all, it is the honor of the entire Wingert family that's involved here. I may be able to persuade the old gentleman to be more reasonable."

"You'd be wasting your breath," the general told him flatly. "I intend to deny everything."

Sir Henry looked up from the short, squat figure of the general to his nephew's larger one, clad in puce satin and adorned with ruby fobs and rings. "I suppose there'd be no harm in it," he said slowly. "There's no way he can escape except past me, and I don't intend to allow that. Come with me, Miss Traherne. I'm certain you'd like some respite from this company."

To Elizabeth's surprise, she found that her hand was trembling as she placed it on Sir Henry's comforting arm. With an uncomfortable backward glance at the short, evil form of the traitorous general, she accompanied Sir Henry through the door and down the first flight of winding stairs.

"I'm sorry you had to see that," Sir Henry said frankly. "Though no doubt you brought it on yourself. We've all warned you to keep out of it. Young Jeremy has been livid. First you interfere with young Fraser's rendezvous with him, you entice Simpkin into revealing classified information, you snoop and pry and nearly get yourself murdered." Sir Henry shook his head reprovingly.

"But why didn't you tell me?" Elizabeth demanded. "Why didn't Jeremy let us know he was home and safe?"

"Women can't keep secrets," Sir Henry said flatly, never knowing how close to death he had come at that moment. Elizabeth controlled the strong urge to push him down the stairs with great effort.

"Did you tell Sumner?" She managed to keep her voice level.

"Jeremy said he'd be even more indiscreet than you," Sir Henry said tactlessly. "You should understand, Miss Traherne, that your brother Jeremy is one of my three best agents; St. Ives and Fraser being the other two. He's been in charge of the French end of this whole nasty affair, and he finally smuggled himself back into the country two weeks ago to oversee the conclusion. He could hardly spare the time for family visits. I could only hope it would be a more satisfactory ending. I'm afraid Wingert is correct in his supposition. The charges won't stick if we don't find the papers. This may all have been for nothing."

"But Jeremy—"

"You may ask him all the questions you want once he gets back from London," Sir Henry said benevolently. "He'll be going straight there to make his report, but then he'll be mustered out and sent home, I should think. He's served above and beyond the call of duty."

"Thank God," she breathed, her eyes bright with joy. "And he'll stay home?"

"I wouldn't guarantee that," Sir Henry replied temporizing. "He was quite taken with a young lady in London, and there's been talk of a match between the two of them. The lady happens to be my daughter," he added sheepishly, and allowed himself to be enveloped in a jubilant embrace. "Not that he won't give his father-in-law a severe dressing down for allowing his sister to get involved in such dangerous activities."

"Oh, he won't blame you," she said confidently. "He knows me too well to think anyone could keep me in line."

"Well, I only hope you've learned your—what in the name of all that's holy was that?"

Elizabeth's normally ruddy color had paled. "It sounded somewhat like a . . . a scream, sir."

"But where did it come from?"

"Directly outside the wall here," she choked out.

At that moment Adolphus's portly figure appeared at the top of the stairs, an affable expression on his round face as he minced toward them. "I'm afraid my uncle was overcome with guilt."

"I beg your pardon?" Sir Henry gasped.

"I pointed out how grievously wrong he'd been in pursuing his recent course, and he decided that the gentlemanly thing to do was to put an end to it."

"An end?"

"Over the parapet," Adolphus elaborated cheerfully. "A tragedy, of course, but really quite a neat solution to all our problems, don't you think?"

"I didn't know suicides screamed when they jumped," Elizabeth said slowly, and Adolphus favored her with a benign smile while picking an imaginary speck of lint from his puce overcoat with ominously scratched hands.

"I am certain that in the normal run of things they don't," he told her. "However, Uncle was, despite everything, a Wingert, and they can be expected to do the unexpected. I can only hope," he continued without any real feeling, "that he didn't land on Captain Fraser. That would be rather a case of killing two birds with one general, don't you think?" With a light laugh he sauntered past the two horror-struck listeners.

"Michael," Elizabeth gasped.

"Don't worry, Miss Traherne," Sir Henry said in a distracted tone. "Fraser's dodged French bullets and swords for the past seven years without much more than a scratch; I doubt one small general would be more difficult to avoid."

"Did Adolphus really . . ." The words failed her, and Sir Henry nodded slowly.

"There seems to be little doubt that he actually did. Just as I've always suspected he saw to LeBoeuf himself. The Wingerts are an odd bunch when it comes right down to it. I suppose I should go apprise my men of the situation. The men won't like it."

"I expect they already know." Adolphus's light voice floated up toward them from further down the winding stairs. "I'll be with m'mother. Have to break the news to her about poor old Uncle. She'll be distraught." The voice faded in the distance.

The two of them went down the dangerous, winding stairs a great deal more slowly than their affable host, holding on to each other for a small kind of creature comfort. The contessa met them at the bottom of the stairs, a question in her dark eyes.

"It's over, Lonnie," Sir Henry said heavily. "Sir Maurice

jumped from the parapet."

"That's not what Michael said," the contessa observed. "He saw two figures struggling up there while he was looking for the papers. Someone threw him over. Was it you, sir?"

"Don't be idiotic!" snapped Sir Henry, his usually even temper finally succumbing to the stress of the evening.

"I'm afraid it was Dolph," Elizabeth said in hushed tones.

"Sir Adolphus?" the contessa echoed. "Well, I'm impressed. I wouldn't have thought Adolphus was that much of a man."

"Contessa!" Elizabeth shrieked. "He murdered his uncle for nothing more than family pride."

"Well, it does tidy things up nicely," she pointed out callously, and Elizabeth shuddered.

"Did they find the papers?" Sir Henry interrupted them.

"Oh, yes. Rupert told me to tell you he has them safe. He and Michael are overseeing the removal of the body right now. Quite messy, I'm afraid. You'll want to avoid the east courtyard, Miss Traherne."

"I would like nothing more than to avoid everything and everybody in this wretched place," she said crossly, and then, with an uncharacteristic display of emotion, promptly burst into tears. A moment later she found herself enveloped in the contessa's perfumed arms. She allowed herself to be led down the hallway to the dubious haven of her room, with the soft voice murmuring soothing sounds all the while. With deft hands her comforter helped her undress, wash her scrapes and bruises, and climb wearily and weepily into the big soft bed.

"I'll tell everyone that you don't wish to be bothered. I don't wonder that it's been a shock to you, and that fool must have run off without even stopping to see how you were," she observed, having missed nothing of Elizabeth's varied and tearful complaints and immediately fastening on the most offensive of the lot. "But you know how men are, my dear. They never think."

"But that's just the trouble," Elizabeth wailed. "I don't know how men are."

"Well, take it from an expert. They're all rag-mannered and idiotic and not worth half the trouble they cause. And that includes Michael Fraser. You'll be well rid of him." This last she offered in the way of an experiment and was well satisfied with Elizabeth's reaction.

Elizabeth's response was to bury her head in her pillow, howling with misery. The contessa placed a comforting hand on her shoulder. "Don't worry, Elizabeth. Everything will be just fine in the end. I realize you feel wretched right now, but by tomorrow morning you'll feel more the thing Trust me."

"The only thing that will make me feel better," came the damp, muffled reply, "is Michael Fraser's head on a platter."

Reassured as to the fondness of Elizabeth's feelings, the contessa took her departure, making her way directly to Fraser's side with a great deal of interesting advice. Elizabeth fell into a deep and mercifully dreamless sleep.

Chapter 18

Monday

ELIZABETH AWOKE late the next morning full of aches, crotchets, and a great sense of ill usage. The sight of her reflection did nothing at all to dispel her mood of gloom. Across one cheekbone was a bruise of a startling purple hue, which had doubtless come when she'd collapsed so gracelessly on the stone parapet. The back of her head still ached from the blow of her unknown assailant, and her stomach rumbled with hunger. It was already past nine, and she hadn't eaten since the noon meal the day before.

With any luck, she told herself crossly as she dressed with hasty movements, Michael Fraser would be long gone with the morning light, and she wouldn't have to see the wretched creature ever again. And Jeremy was back! That one brief look was scarcely enough. Michael Fraser would be easy enough to ignore if Jeremy was still there. At least some good had come of all this.

As for the rest of this miserable houseparty, the sooner she was gone from this ghastly place, the better. She wasted an extra ten minutes making her thick chestnut hair fall in its most attractive arrangement, disdained to powder her magnificent bruise, and made her way downstairs to the smaller library at the front of the house. With a great deal of presence she seated herself at a card table, summoned a servant, and requested that coffee and cinnamon buns be brought to her in her hideaway. The parlor maid, somewhat used to the oddness of the house and its inhabitants by this time, hastily did her bidding without more than one or two curious glances and then hastened to inform the master of the house and his breakfast guests where the final member of the houseparty was to be found.

She was well into her second game of patience when Sumner and a glowing Brenna appeared in the doorway. "Wish us happy, Elizabeth," Sumner ordered in mellow tones. "Brenna has condescended to make me the happiest man in the world."

"Well, if she has already done so, I fail to see why you need my wishes," Elizabeth observed irritably. "It's her that will be needing all the help, having to put up with the likes of you."

"Sumner is the best of all men," Brenna said in misty tones, convincing Elizabeth for once and all that love must surely be blind.

"Well, I am delighted. This has been far too long in coming," she said, struggling to say all the proper things despite her own black humor. "Have you set a date for the wedding?"

"As soon as Jeremy returns, we shall. This dreadful business with Sir Maurice has overset everyone, and we felt it would be ill-mannered of us at the moment," Brenna said smoothly, before Sumner could reply.

"Where has Jeremy gone off to?" Elizabeth demanded, news of his defection setting the seal on her foul temper. "I barely had a chance to see him last night."

"And he's not very pleased with you, I must say," Sumner pontificated. "You'd best expect a rare dressing down once he returns."

"Returns from where?" she questioned, keeping a tight leash on her temper.

"London. He and Rupert took off at first light. Sir Henry's orders, I gather."

"How nice," Elizabeth said listlessly, refusing to ask the question that most exercised her mind. "I'm very glad he's safely back and very happy for the two of you." She rose from her seat and embraced the Irish girl with unfeigned enthusiasm. "Welcome to the family, Brenna. I know Jeremy will feel the same."

"Thank you, Elizabeth," Brenna replied smoothly. "And I want you to know that you will always be a welcome guest in our home."

Elizabeth looked startled for a moment, then smiled, silently applauding her future sister-in-law's adroitness. "I'm sure you'll see to that," she responded, with only a trace of mischief.

"We're going down to the manse so that Brenna can have a look at her new house. She'll want to make changes, spruce the old place up a bit, make it more habitable," Sumner continued, with a fond look at his chosen one. Elizabeth, who previously had considered the manse to be more than presentable, bit her tongue. "We're taking the trap. You don't mind waiting until I bring Brenna back? The trap's rather crowded with three people."

Elizabeth minded a great deal. "Perhaps Lady Elfreda will lend me a carriage?" she suggested, not putting any reliance on the notion.

"Her ladyship's gone into seclusion. Perfectly natural, of course. She's sustained a double shock, losing her brother-in-law like that and then losing Brenna," Sumner said solemnly. "I wouldn't bother her with trivialities at a time like this, Elizabeth. It surely is not too great an importunity to ask you to allow my affianced and myself a few hours of privacy."

"No, of course not," she said with a sigh.

"That reminds me, Elizabeth," Sumner said, tearing his besotted gaze from his glowing bride to be. "Rupert asked me to give you his regards and to tell you he will have something to ask you when he returns. I had the oddest feeling that he might be planning to make you an offer."

"You think so?" she inquired dully, surveying the cards laid out in front of her with unseeing eyes.

"It seemed very much that way. How delightfully everything is working out! I shall see if I can persuade him to come up to scratch. I'm sure it will please Jeremy."

"I have no intention of marrying Rupert," Elizabeth said stonily.

Sumner laughed an indulgent little laugh, one he reserved for the foibles of the weaker sex. "I'm certain that's why Rupert left so early this morning. He and Jeremy were thick as thieves, and I have little doubt he'll ask permission to pay his respects to you, Elizabeth. You should be very grateful at this unexpected offer. Even though Captain Fraser isn't a villain after all, he's hardly likely to offer marriage. Apparently this was all some part he was playing, though I'm not entirely convinced, even now."

"Sumner, dearest, you know that Sir Henry told us he's actually a very nice young man. Well liked, respected, and with a comfortable fortune behind him. Not really your sort at all, Elizabeth." There was a malicious gleam in the green cat's eyes, and Elizabeth decided then and there never to trust another woman.

Sumner gazed fatuously upon his beloved before turning his gaze upon his recalcitrant sister. "You really should jump at the chance Rupert's offering you. If you have any sense," he added, his voice expressing strong doubts that she was thus endowed.

"If I had any sense, I would," she agreed gloomily, and returned to her card game much disheartened as the young lovers took themselves off.

Her next visitor was somewhat more welcome but equally disturbing. "I just came to wish you good-bye and Godspeed," Sir Henry said, smiling benevolently down on her. "I hope you aren't suffering any ill effects from your adventures last evening."

"Apart from a headache, a disfigured countenance, and a supremely bad temper, I am simply thriving."

"Well, you know, it all worked out for the best. It would have been extremely difficult to make any charges stick against the general. He was a trickster from way back. This war might have ended years earlier without the interference of men like him."

"And Adolphus is going to get away with cold-blooded murder?" she questioned sharply. "Nothing is going to happen to him after he assisted his uncle off the parapet?"

"I'm afraid not. There's no proof of that, either, and it's rid the Crown of a fairly sticky problem. The populace wouldn't have taken too kindly to a general selling secrets to the Frenchies. No, we're better off all around this way. I know you might wish for revenge, seeing as how it was Sir Adolphus who clubbed you on the head and locked you in his uncle's closet, but—"

"Adolphus?" she shrieked in disbelief. "But why?"

"Despite what he says, he knew as well as anyone what his uncle was up to. I gather LeBoeuf was somewhat indiscreet before he . . . ahem . . . died. Adolphus was hoping to avoid any trouble by seeing to his uncle himself. That involved keeping everyone else blind to the goings-on, including your curious little self. He told me he greatly regretted the need for violence upon your person."

"Did he, now?" she snarled, slapping the cards down on the table with unnecessary vehemence. "I'd like to show him what violence is."

"I would suggest, Miss Traherne, that the less said about the events of the last few days, the better. I know Jeremy would agree with me. It would be in everyone's best interests if you simply rose above your justifiable provocation and ignored Sir Adolphus's assault. He said he hit you as gently as he could."

"Thoughtful of him," she observed cynically.

"I can trust in your discretion in this matter?" There was a hint of steel beneath Sir Henry's light tones, and Elizabeth nodded reluctantly.

"That's the girl." He placed a paternal kiss on her unbruised cheek. "Well, I just wanted to say good-bye and to tell you that I couldn't be more delighted. Michael's been like a son to Lady Beatrice and myself." And with those cryptic words he bowed himself out of the room before Elizabeth could do more than stare in bewilderment.

Elizabeth turned back to the neglected game of patience, with all the patience she herself could muster. She was allowed a mere three minutes of peace before Lady Elfreda, whose deep seclusion had begun to pall, tottered into the room on unsteady feet, dressed in flowing black crepe, her basilisk eyes red-rimmed from weeping.

"There you are, missy," she said in waspish tones. "I suppose you're pleased with yourself, eh?"

"What do you mean?"

"Matchmaking for that lily-livered brother of yours and my Brenna. I had her picked for Adolphus!"

"I really don't think they would have suited," she said gently. "I am sorry about your brother-in-law, Lady Elfreda," she added mendaciously, mindful of her duty. "If there is anything I can do, you must let me know."

"You won't like living with Brenna, my girl," Lady Elfreda said, brushing the polite phrases aside. "She has a mind of her own, that one. The vicar'll be living under the cat's paw in no time at all, and you'll simply be in the way. I think you'd best come take Brenna's place with me. I'll need a companion, and you'll need a genteel occupation, eh?" To punctuate the flattering offer, she leaned over and gave her a little pinch.

Elizabeth controlled her start of pain. "I am more than grateful for the thought, Lady Elfreda, but I'm afraid I have other plans," she said in a silken voice. "Jeremy will be back, and I can always keep house for him until he marries. Failing that, my old governess could keep me company when I set up house on my own."

"Sumner mentioned some such nonsense," her ladyship said, dismissing it offhandedly. "He'll never allow you to do any such thing."

"He'll have no say in the matter. I have little doubt that Brenna will be more than happy to see me settled elsewhere."

"You'll be sorry you threw away a chance like this, Elizabeth Traherne. And don't think I'll change my mind and have you when you're destitute and disgraced!"

"I have no intention of being either, thank you. Good-bye, Lady Elfreda. I've had a simply delightful time these last few days, but I think I shan't repeat the experience."

The old woman stared at her, her pale, lined face mottled with rage. "Impertinence!" she fumed before striding out of the room, nearly colliding with the contessa on her way in.

The elegant black-clad figure watched the old lady storm away, then turned her lively dark eyes back to Elizabeth. "Do you mind if I join you?"

"It wouldn't do me any good if I did," she said bitterly. "Everyone seems to have it in mind."

"You've seen Michael this morning?" she inquired, obviously surprised.

"Everyone but Michael Fraser," Elizabeth amended irritably. "At least I've been spared that."

"I was startled because I thought I saw him leave a short while ago. No doubt he's coming back before he takes off for Sussex."

"He's going to Sussex?" Elizabeth questioned idly, suddenly intent on the forgotten card game.

"To his parents' place. A lovely spot, I hear, though Michael's estate in Kent is every bit as pretty, although somewhat smaller, Sir Henry tells me. For a younger son Michael is quite well off."

"How felicitous for him," Elizabeth said sourly.

The contessa smiled, greatly amused. "I came in to tell you that Adolphus and I plan to be wed next month. Just a small ceremony, since he, of course, is in mourning. We hoped you might be my maid of honor."

She stared at the contessa's irrepressible face in amazement. "You must be funning! After what he did?"

"Oh, I shan't mind that. Most of the men I've been attracted to have a murderous streak. And none of them have been half so well-off. I intend to enjoy myself fully as Lady Wingert."

"I only hope you won't regret it."

"That's what Michael says. But I assure you, I shan't. I'm getting too old to racket around the world. The war will be over before too long. It won't take much to capture the Corsican monster this time, and let us hope they keep him someplace where he can't escape so easily. Wish me happy?"

"I wish you luck," Elizabeth said firmly. "You'll need that more."

"Unhandsome of you, Lizzie. You don't mind if I call you that, do you? I heard Michael use it, and I must say it suits you."

"It would do me little good if I did mind," she said wearily.

"True enough." The contessa laughed with what Elizabeth considered to be heartless merriment. "Well, I wish you all the happiness in the world. Lord knows, you deserve it almost as much as I do." And she sailed out of the room, leaving Elizabeth in doubtful peace once more.

Disconsolately she rose, strolling over to the window. Years ago, months ago, even days ago, she would have viewed the prospect of an offer from Rupert St. Ives with unalloyed joy. Now the mere thought filled her heart with the deepest depression. The thought that Jeremy was actually home, safe at last, brought a temporary lightening to her mood, only to be sunk in gloom once more at the insistent memory of Michael Fraser.

Michael Fraser, who had been acting a part for the better portion of a year. Pretending to be a traitor, a gambler, a ne'er-do-well. Pretending to care for her, when all the time he was merely doing his duty. All his "my loves" and "when we're marrieds" were of a piece with his dangerous image. All fabrication.

And she had been a complete, utter, blind, infatuated fool. How he must have been laughing at her as he lied to her, played with her, kissed her, and then abandoned her. There was nothing Elizabeth wanted more than to crawl away and hide. She was too furious and embarrassed to ever want to see Michael Fraser again. It was fortunate he had felt a complete lack of interest, she told herself, and had taken off so that she could still retain the shreds of a much assaulted dignity. If she ever saw Michael Fraser again, she told herself stormily, she would nod coolly and walk on by. Not by any action on her part would he know that her heart was irrevocably shattered. She stared gloomily out the leaded glass windows to the front drive, contemplating a future filled with noble suffering.

A very large, elegant coach was waiting by the front entrance, piled high with trunks and valises and pulled by a perfectly matched set of bay horses. It took Elizabeth a few moments to realize that the trunks on top of the coach looked familiar and a few moments more to realize that they were hers. In a blind fury she strode into the hall only to careen into Michael Fraser.

"What are my trunks doing on that coach?" she demanded furiously, disentangling herself with a stifled pang of regret. "Where did they come from?"

"The manse," he replied, a faint smile playing around his

mouth. In the light of day he appeared surprisingly lighthearted, the sapphire blue eyes smiling down at her, the grim planes of his tanned face relaxed and happy. "Brenna packed them for me."

"I'm sure she did," Elizabeth said bitterly. "Whatever for?"

"Well, I'd be more than happy to take you without a stitch on your back, but I thought you'd be more comfortable visiting my family with your wardrobe intact."

"Who says I am visiting your family?" she demanded in dangerous tones.

Surprisingly enough for an experienced soldier, Fraser failed to recognize his peril. "I do. I wrote them to expect us when I sent for the carriage. They're very eager to meet you, and Jeremy will be coming along in a few days, as well. He approves, you know."

"Approves of what? Not of your high-handed ways, I hope," she said in a dampening tone of voice. "And why should I meet your parents?"

His dazzling smile left her stonily unmoved. "Don't you think they deserve to meet my future wife?"

Her temper exploded once more. "How dare you?" she fumed. "How dare you just assume I would fall into your arms if you merely beckoned! You certainly have a high opinion of yourself, Captain Fraser, if you think you're such a catch for every unattached female."

"I would think you'd be far happier with me than with Brenna the Beastly. Poor Sumner is already looking a bit downtrodden."

"Oh, of course. Nothing could be more delightful than traipsing around Europe as you got yourself into one scrape after another! A spy is just my idea of a perfect husband."

"Well, actually this was my last assignment. In another week I'll be out of the army, and then I might stand for Parliament. You know you'd make an admirable politician's wife with your infinite tact."

"Ooooh," she fumed. "Well, difficult as it may be to believe, I find I must decline your flattering offer that was never even made. I have other plans!"

Fraser seemed amused by her rage. "Would you like me to go down on one knee, Lizzie? I thought we understood each other tolerably well. It's not every female I kiss in closets."

"I would like you, Captain Fraser, to go to the devil!"

"What is all this unseemly noise?" Lady Elfreda's stentorian tenor bellowed down the hall. "Doesn't anyone know how to behave in a house of mourning?"

Both combatants ignored the plaintive question. By this time Fraser was furious, too, and his eyes blazed down into hers. "You are being extremely tiresome, Lizzie," he said evenly. "Do you or do you not wish to come with me?"

"If you won't pay any heed to what I've been saying, perhaps this will serve to convince you," she cried, and slapped him across the face with all her strength.

The sound echoed shockingly in the cavernous hall. Fraser stared down at her, unmoved. "If it's physical violence you prefer," he said, and scooped her up, tossing her over his shoulder and carrying her thrashing figure toward the door.

"Put me down this instant!"

"When we get to Sussex," he replied calmly, carrying her out the front door into the damp spring air. The carriage door was already open, and he tossed her inside with an enthusiastic lack of gentleness, following behind her and slamming the door. As she struggled to gain her balance, the coach pulled away, sending her toppling into Fraser's waiting arms.

"How dare you?" she demanded hotly, her eyes straying guiltily to the red imprint of her hand on his tanned cheek.

"I would suggest you watch your step with me, Lizzie," he drawled, a light in his usually somber eyes. "I can be quite ruthless when I need to be."

"I'm certain you can be," she snapped. "Including manhandling helpless females."

"Anyone less helpless I am unlikely to see," he protested. "However, I must confess you were absolutely right in your earlier supposition. I did bash poor Brenna on the head and then come and ply you with sweet words and kisses. To which you responded admirably."

"You didn't!" she gasped, barely managing to stifle the reluctant giggle at the thought of sour Brenna's downfall. "But why?"

"Because I didn't want her wandering around the east tower any more than I wished you to," he said simply.

"You could have kissed her, too," Elizabeth offered. "That would have distracted her."

"But I had no desire to kiss Brenna. Only you, my love. So tell me, would you prefer to have the coachman leave you off at the vicarage?" he asked coolly, his arms nevertheless tight around her unresisting body.

"I dislike above all things having my mind made up for me," she muttered sulkily, trying to preserve her rage while clinging to his shoulders.

"Then by all means make it up yourself," he offered generously, one long-fingered hand straying beneath her willful chin. "Would you like to go back to the vicarage, or would you like to come to Sussex and meet my family?"

"Why should I meet your family?" she demanded in a gentler voice as his other hand tightened around her slender waist.

"Gad, you can be delectably tiresome at times," he sighed, nibbling her earlobe in a distracting fashion. She made no effort to wriggle out of the way. "Because you are going to marry me, like it or no, and—"

She tore herself out of his arms, landing with a solid thump on the carriage floor. "I will not be told what to do!" she declared thunderously, ignoring her ignominious position.

She was also unaware of how completely endearing she was, sitting there in her rumpled blue velvet dress, her tawny chestnut hair falling down around her shoulders, her sherry-colored eyes bright with suspicion, and the bruise across one cheekbone. Fraser smiled.

"Will you, my luscious, delectable termagant, marry the poor fool who sits before you completely besotted, and rescue him from a life of loneliness and despair?"

Elizabeth considered him for a long moment. "Why?" she

asked simply for what she told herself would be positively the last time.

Without further ado Michael pulled her willing form back into his arms, settling her comfortably against his shoulder. "Because I love you," he said, and proceeded to take unfair advantage of her by kissing her quite ruthlessly.

When he finally allowed, her to breathe, Elizabeth decided that such an overbearing tyrant had best be humored. "In that case," she murmured dreamily, "I will."

The End

About the Author

Anne Stuart is currently celebrating forty years as a published novelist. She has won every major award in the romance field and appeared on the *NYT* Bestseller List, *Publisher's Weekly*, and *USA Today*. Anne Stuart currently lives in northern Vermont.

Printed in Great Britain
by Amazon